White Lilies Lagoon

Janina Raven

White Lilies Lagoon

A Fantasy Thriller

© 2022 Janina Nilges
Herstellung und Verlag: BoD – Books on Demand, Norderstedt
ISBN: 9783756225736

HEADQUARTERS
Sparrow

Nevada Morrigane clung to a windowsill, twenty meters above a crowded highway. The moon threw silvery rays on her as she balanced on a small ledge on the wall, reaching for the screwdriver from her belt in a dangerous attempt to open the window one-handedly.

"Wouldn't it be a better idea if I did this?" I suggested for the tenth time, but she shook her head.

"I swear, if you fall-"

"I won't fall, Birdie. It's not the first time I'm doing this."

"But it's the first time in years." I sighed and changed my pose from cross-legged levitation to standing in the air to have a better chance at catching her if she fell. I mean, it was my *mother*. Double my age, of course not double my weight, but just as tall as me. Which meant *really* tall.

I'd have low chances of saving her.

"There we go." The window swung open to the inside and Mum turned to me with a satisfied smile. "Welcome to the Army headquarters."

I followed her inside the room – a library apparently. Rain, who sat on my shoulder, nibbled my ear as we both looked around.

It was a surprise nobody had seen us from the highway – it wasn't quite the least suspicious thing to break into the ninth floor of an old villa right next to the city's most important street – and it was also a surprise Mum had opened that window with nothing but a screwdriver.

"That isn't a normal tool, is it?"

"Absolutely not." She laughed. "A handy leftover from my army time. Just like this one." She put the screwdriver back into her belt and pulled out a gun instead.

"Sorry?" I raised my eyebrows. "I thought there weren't any guards here tonight!"

"Just virtual ones. Which is why we wouldn't have stood any chance getting in here via the stairway. The cameras all point towards the doors. Except for one." She gestured me to stay where I was, near the window, and carefully stepped forward, between the shelves.

I didn't even realise she'd fired a shot at first because it was so quiet. When Mum waved me to get closer, my gaze met the splotch of red paint dripping off something over the door on the opposite wall.

"What the heck?" I grinned.

"Oh, just their own weapons I'm using against them now." She gave me a nervous smile. "Alright, you know what we are looking for?"

"Proof that what Cecily said is wrong." I shivered as I remembered what Thorne's and my ex-landlady had claimed to know two weeks ago. That the army had been in the wrong for killing the Wicked Magicians. That they had been innocent all along. And thus, that Mum had murdered people who never did anything evil.

"Or that it is right." Mum stopped analysing one of the shelves and turned back to me. "We should be prepared for the possibility that she is telling the truth."

"No way. No way, you can't be-"

"Guilty?" Mum let out a bitter laugh. "Sparrow, I am guilty anyway. I have killed people, no matter if it was for a good cause or not. I am guilty. I just have to find out if-"

"If you were in the right?" I cut her off sharply. "And what if you weren't? What if Cecily *did* tell the truth, as you just said? Then you're gonna drown yourself in regrets and self-hatred? Don't you think it'd be better if you didn't know?"

"Some truths shouldn't be kept secret." Mum turned away again. "Whether I want to or not, that doesn't matter. We owe the truth to the whole world. Especially to the Wickeds, in case they were right. The government would need to act."

I didn't know what to say, so I just wandered off between the shelves.

"Look, Rain," I said and the unicorn squirrel jumped onto one of the shelves and looked at me as if he understood every word I said. I didn't doubt he actually did. "Isn't it funny how the Magic Army has noted down all their missions on paper in fear of being hacked, and now we are here anyway, being able to read through every single member's biography and all the-"

"Sparrow?" My mum's voice sounded distressed. "You need to come here immediately. I found something."

～ 🕷 ～

Thorne

"Thorne?"

"What's the matter this time?" I could hardly suppress an annoyed groan. Jasmine had kept me up all night again. *Again*, as she had so often in the last two weeks, ever since we all moved in with Sparrow's parents.

"I'm scared."

I'm scared as well, my girlfriend and her mother are risking their freedom with some illegal action while we are all being hunted by some cruel magical killers! I just sighed. "They will welcome you. I know it."

"But what if they don't? I don't remember anything about them! What if I have changed too much?"

"I can reassure you, you haven't changed at all."

She must have heard the amusement in my voice, but she didn't comment on it. She was probably too busy making up terrible outcomes for tomorrow, when she was going to meet her parents for the first time in over a year. For the first time since last year's summer solstice, to be exact. Since she died.

"Would you maybe..." She sounded reluctant. "Come with me?"

I sat up straight on my mattress and reached for the light switch. Brightness flooded the room and from her face, I could tell that she was dead serious.

"Why the heck should I come with you?" I asked.

"Because I'm nervous."

"Sparrow and I have school tomorrow. You know that."

"Maybe you can skip? The teachers won't mind if you take a day off. Nevada could call in sick for you." Jasmine tilted her head. "And Sparrow can go alone for once. You and I, we are friends too, after all!"

Are we really? I wasn't too sure. We had never really been friends; she had abandoned us several times. All we were right now was roommates.

"Maybe we are friends, but Sparrow is my girlfriend. And maybe I don't even want to skip school, no matter if the teachers will mind or not!" Slowly, the general tiredness took over the aggression level in my body. Why couldn't she just let me sleep? Wasn't it enough I had to worry about Sparrow and Nemo?

I sank back onto my pillow but sat up straight again when I heard the front door open and close again. Two silent voices, then a third, all getting louder, then somebody knocked at Sparrow's bedroom.

"Yeah?" Jasmine said.

Why did she even- It's not my home, but hers even less!

"We are back." *Sparrow.* She came in and sat down next to me, on her own mattress. Rain jumped from her shoulder and into his little bed on the window sill. "And we've got news."

"Good or bad news?" I asked.

"That depends on your point of view." Nemo followed her daughter inside, and Mortimer closed the door behind the three.

"You will never guess what we found out," Sparrow said slowly.

"The Wickeds were never evil?" I guessed. "Cecily was right?"

"Cecily was right." Nemo sounded bitter when she confirmed my assumption. "The whole army was wrong. We were told the wrong things."

"But they performed evil rites!" I hesitated. "Or didn't they?"

"They didn't." Nemo took a deep breath. "In one of the secret, coded files, the whole case got resolved and then was hidden to keep the peace. Imagine if someone found out how wrong we have been all this time—" She let out a bitter laugh, then added in a serious voice, "they *will* find out, I will personally assure that."

"Now tell us what happened," Mortimer pressed for more information.

"When I uncoded the document, it said that proof was provided by army troops that searched the abandoned lairs of the Wickeds," Nevada explained. "One of the magic powers of the army leader is to sense lies. After the inquiry of some Wickeds, he got sceptical about their true intentions, but didn't make anything public and only started to gather information after the war. And after the proof was examined, they found out the truth. What we had been told to be rites... it actually was medicine. They worked on a drug to cure cancer and similar fatal illnesses. And the army leader kept everything to himself, just to not cause a catastrophic reveal in the army. How inhumane—" Nemo took another deep breath. "And the worst thing... In that file, it was also mentioned who gave our army leaders the wrong hints that caused the war. It was Thill Holmwood."

War Awaits
Sparrow

I couldn't hold back a smile when I saw Dad, Thorne and Jasmine's astounded faces. Yeah, they were relatable. Mum and I had probably had the same expression when we'd read the lines in that secret file Mum had decoded.

"Thill Holmwood, aka Thill LeDoux?" Thorne repeated, as if we weren't talking about his uncle.

"Absolutely." Mum nodded. "And from that, we can assume that it was his mission to put the Wickeds up against the Army."

"So the Eternals–" Thorne frowned. "The Eternals, I mean the LeDouxes and their friends, have put the Wickeds up against the Army?"

"Shouldn't you know about this?" I froze when I realised it. "Weren't you one of them, back then?"

Thorne lowered his head. "I never really was one of them. They never told me anything. Maybe– maybe they were afraid of me."

"What do you mean?"

"Thill and Estelle–" Thorne shook his head. "I don't even remember. It's been a long time. They had a daughter; her name was Lilith. I didn't understand back then, because I didn't know there was a life outside the estate and I thought what this family did was normal. She tried to overthrow them. Become even stronger and more evil than them. And they-" He looked up. "They killed her. That's why I know that the grimoire can kill them."

"They killed their own daughter?" Jasmine's voice broke.

"It was Clarisse's idea." Thorne sighed. "And I think after that, they decided it's too dangerous to have kids that know about things. Ethan – he was just a new-born. Clarisse gave Rosary the choice to kill him or let him partake in the rite, so he'd never grow up."

"He's been a new-born for hundreds of years?" Dad shook his head. "They are insane."

"Yes." Mum reached for her phone. "But more importantly, they are *dangerous*. They are putting the Wickeds up against the army again. The whole meeting two weeks ago, I assume it was only the beginning. The only way to prevent another war is to make all this official. The government, the army, they have to talk to the Wickeds. Apologize. Pay compensations." She hastily typed out a message to someone. "I need to have a bunch of video chats now, and you should try to catch some sleep."

Mum was on TV the next day. And of course, we had cancelled everything. The school appointment, Jasmine's meeting with her parents, Mum and Dad going to work. It was all too dangerous; nobody knew how the Eternals and the Wickeds would react. Or the army, after we broke into their headquarters and revealed their darkest secret – that they had attempted to hide what could be considered genocide. Who was even on our side now?

The phone hadn't been silent for a second since the first news show at 5am.

Nevada Nemo Morrigane reveals horrific secrets of the Arcane Wars!

Were the Arcane Wars justified?

Were the Wicked Magicians innocent?

Headlines flooded the internet and the shows on different channels, all talking about Mum.

Not about me. She had revealed the entire truth, her reasons for breaking into the headquarters, how she found the files. All she had left out was that she hadn't been alone. She wanted to keep me safe while taking full responsibility for her actions.

"You know what?" Mum sighed. "I made another mistake. We haven't got *anybody* on our side now. Everybody could be willing to kill us now."

"Even the army?" Jasmine stared at her.

"Even the army." Mum cleared her throat. "The Wickeds might now officially want to take revenge. The Eternals hate us anyway. And the army – sometimes, they decide that one member less is better than one revelation more. Especially because I'm not a real member anymore. Especially because their leader has always hated me in a way."

"But will this all prevent the war?" Dad asked.

"I have zero clue." She massaged her temples. "Either the government apologizes and the Wickeds accept it, or the government apologizes and the Wickeds don't accept it, or– Ah, there are so many possibilities!" She shook her head. "I'm scared."

This – these two words – were worse than anything she'd said until now. Mum, scared? That was impossible.

"So what you said…" Thorne asked carefully. "At the event, were there Wickeds? Or were they normal people?"

"Both." Mum sighed. "That's why I think it's only the beginning. They assembled a bunch of Wickeds and *normal* magicians, that's insane! Thorne, can you imagine them teaming up with who they consider lesser people?"

Thorne slowly shook his head, but she spoke on already. "They are assembling the Wickeds that surrendered back then, and also normal magicians! They are forming an army! And we cannot even leave the house because everybody wants to kill us!" She jumped up and went to the window. "I am going insane here."

"Mum..."

"Yeah?" She turned back to me, now back to normal.

"Nothing. I'm just... worried." I sighed.

"We all are." She returned and took my hands. "Promise me you won't leave the house."

"Are you leaving?" I gave her a worried look.

"No, of course not. But if something should happen... You're safe here. In an emergency, lock yourself up in the safe room. Get weapons. You know how to use them."

Yeah, we all did. She had insisted on giving Thorne and Jasmine lessons with shotguns.

"Mum, but you don't think~"

The doorbell rang.

We all froze, stared at each other, and eventually, Mum got up, grabbed her revolver from the living room table and went into the hallway.

I didn't even dare to breathe. Who could it be? The Eternals? Cecily? Or what if she was only holding some poor post officer at gunpoint now?

"Somebody please bring me gloves," she yelled across the house and I jumped up to grab the gardening gloves Dad had left on the shelf near the terrace door.

"What do you need them f-" I almost choked on the question. Mum was kneeling in front of an envelope that lay on the doormat. "What *is* that?"

"A letter."

"I can see that myself."

"I can see just as much as you, Sparrow." She sounded distressed as she took the gloves and put them on to pick up the letter. "Now close the door and lock it."

I did as I was told and followed her back into the living room.

"Nobody was outside," she told the others. "Just this letter. I'm afraid it might be poisoned. Poison was one of my favourite weapons, wouldn't that be the perfect way to kill me?" she added in a fragile voice.

"Don't drown in paranoia, Nemo," Dad said. "Open it."

Thorne flinched at Dad's rough tone, but I knew Mum needed his harsh note to get back to what she really was. Bold and fearless.

"Alright." She nodded and opened the envelope to unfold the paper inside. She read through it, the held it out for us to read.

Nemo,

Meet me tonight, midnight, at the place where we fought our last battle.

What you have done needs to be talked through. Just you and me.

C.

"Cecily," Thorne said.

"Of course."

"Or Clarisse?" Jasmine said, but Mum shook her head. "Clarisse doesn't talk things through. She just kills."

"Are you gonna go?" Dad asked.

Mum laughed. She just laughed.

"That's a yes, Mrs. Morrigane?" Jasmine carefully asked.

"That is a yes, Jasmine." Mum closed her eyes and dropped down in an armchair. "Whether I risk my life here or there, what does it matter?"

Jasmine

I n the late afternoon, as we watched the tenth news show for the day, there was a change.

"Two letters reached us half an hour ago, both sent by the Wicked Magicians," the news reporter said. "Apparently, they have split up into two parties. Half wants to keep out of everything, especially the war that has been threatening the Magicals and thus the whole country for the past two weeks. The other half, however, decided to team up with the Eternals to get revenge for the false accusations." The reporter cleared his throat. "We will keep you updated on everything. For now, all that's left is to hope the war will never start."

"Silly boy." Nemo leant back in her seat. "He has no clue what's really at stake. There is no way to evade that war anymore, not now that the Wickeds have done this. They openly announced their wish for revenge."

❧ 🕷 ❦

The day went by without any further events. Nemo kept us updated on what her boss – the local police boss – got told by the government. She'd decided that, if a war should happen, she would not return to the army. Instead, she would fight with the magical department of the police – and even if she didn't explicitly state it, she was probably hoping to get protection from them in case the army would attack her as well.

The evening came, and Nemo got up from the dinner table. "It's time. We are leaving."

"Excuse me?" Thorne mumbled, still some bread in his mouth, and swallowed hard before adding, "Where are we going, Nemo?"

"To Cecily."

"You're taking us with you?" Sparrow asked.

"She will kill me," Nemo said. "And I need somebody to save me if I fuck up. Which I likely will."

"You've never *fucked up!*" Sparrow stared at her.

"I've fucked up a lot." She sounded tired. "Please accept that. I'm not infallible."

"And where exactly are we going?" I asked.

"To the place where Cecily and I fought our last battle – side by side, back then." Nemo sounded bitter. "And that place is White Lilies Lagoon."

❧ 🕷 ☙

"White Lilies Lagoon?" Sparrow frowned. "That isn't a coincidence, right?"

"Of course not." Her mother nervously cracked her knuckles. "It's a lagoon near the coast at White Lilies Creek."

"Oh, of *course!*" I let out a sarcastic laugh. "Wasn't it clear everything would lead back there?"

Nevada shrugged. "We are leaving now. Put on some dark clothes. Take as many weapons as you can carry."

Rites and Shots
Sparrow

The journey to White Lilies was spent in a painful silence and I missed Rain already, but Dad as vet had assured me the most reasonable thing was to leave him at home.

We'd left the house only after Mum had made sure nobody was there, no snipers anywhere.

That she was driving the car scared me a bit – her hands were shaking and her eyes were straying off the road a bit too often, but she safely knew the way and Dad wasn't too confident he did anymore.

Jasmine, Thorne and I sat squeezed on the backseats, backpacks at our feet and guns on our laps. The cold metal weighed hard on my legs. Mum had said we should save her if she'd fuck up – but would I ever really kill anyone? Cecily?

If I could save Mum with it, I would do it, I was sure.

We passed White Lilies Creek and arrived a few kilometres further in a field at a quarter to midnight. Old, half rotten corn plants awaited us.

The night was starless and foggy as we snuck out of the car. Mum pushed us into the corn field immediately and led us through it – ducked and almost on our knees. Was this really necessary?

Our way led us towards a forest, and as we reached it, Mum straightened her back.

"It's time," she said and pulled her hair up into a bun. "Five minutes left. I will go first, and you will follow at a distance."

"Go *where?*" Thorne asked.

"Mortimer knows the way." Mum gave Dad a short kiss and before I could say anything, she was already gone.

"Where-" Jasmine stared at Dad. "Where did she go?"

"Into the catacombs, where we used to fight." Dad looked away into the distance. Silence.

Something rustled and I spun around, but there was nothing. A thousand eyes seemed to watch us, but factually, we were alone.

Dad nodded. "Let's go."

He took a step forward and only now, I saw the rock in front of us that had iron rungs that led into a hole in the ground.

"I'll go first." I shivered. *Anything is better than staying here in the forest alone.*

I put the weapon into my belt and carefully climbed on the ladder. The rusty stairs bent under my feet as I went lower and lower. Eventually, I stood in a narrow hallway, surrounded by crude white walls, dimly lit by a flickering torch every few metres. I ran my fingers along the walls and analysed the white powder on my fingertips – chalk. These were chalk rock formations.

Jasmine, Thorne and Dad stood next to me only a few minutes later. Dad looked down the hallway, then marched on and we followed him in silence. Every now and then, the tunnel split, went upward or downward, and we followed the lit ways – up to one crossing.

"Quiet now," Dad whispered, even though we hadn't said a single word for minutes.

We took the tunnel that led us upstairs, into the dark. Dad didn't use a flashlight and I was too scared to ask for one. We just walked on through the dark and I kept running my hands across the walls to keep the smallest bit of orientation. If only I had Thorne's power of night vision – I assumed he was able to see without problems.

My fingers suddenly lost track of the walls and I ran into Dad, who'd suddenly stopped, and Jasmine and Thorne ran into me.

"Wh–"

"Shh!" Dad put his hand on my shoulder and led me to where I had thought was another wall, and slowly, I realised we were standing in a very small hall around a hole in the ground.

My eyes slowly got used to the darkness and I saw Dad had knelt down, so I did the same.

Bright light shone up through the hole.

Below us was a round room with a good dozen of tunnels leading to it – and Mum had just come in through one of those, a burning torch in her hand. One by one, she lit the twelve torches on the wall, then threw the torch into one of the tunnels.

Splash.

"There's the sea," Dad whispered.

And then, a second person entered the room.

Cecily.

My hands automatically reached for the revolver from my belt, but I didn't dare to release the catch yet.

The flickering torches threw dancing shadows on the faces of the two fighters below us.

"Cecily," Mum said slowly and opened her coat. She raised her pistol from the inner pocket – and knelt down to put it on the ground!

"Army rite to show you come in peace," Dad whispered while Mum revealed another gun and a knife from her bootleg and a dagger she'd strapped to her hip and hid under her coat.

"Cecily's supposed to do the same now," Dad added slowly.

Cecily smiled. She revealed a pistol, but instead of putting it down, she released the catch and pointed it at Mum's forehead.

"Nevada Morrigane." The first words she spoke, and they were so full of spite. "Finally, I've got you where I've wanted you for years!"

"On my knees, begging for mercy?" Mum let out a bitter laugh and attempted to get up, but Cecily wrapped her finger around the trigger, and Mum sank back to her knees, fear flashing through her eyes.

"You didn't expect that, did you, *Nemo*?" Cecily smiled again. "You're still the same naive girl you were back then. Thinking the army traditions could save you. Thinking you were in the right. There is no right or wrong, Nevada, no black and white. Just a grey blurring mess of good and evil."

"Yeah, and you're a traitor, a double agent." Mum laughed again. "Neither of us is really without guilt, right?"

"Without guilt?" Cecily cried out and her voice pitched. "You are the only guilty one here! You killed innocents!"

Mum flinched. "Listen, Cecily, I know that I have done wrong! The LeDouxes have made me believe things that are wrong! Together, we can stop them."

"You are guilty," Cecily cried again. "You have full responsibility for this! You should have done research, you should have double checked what you were told! But you were just a naive little girl that thought murder could bring action and adventure into her life! You will pay for what you have done!"

"Listen, Cecily~"

A shot, followed by a deafening silence.

"Mortimer, you damned~," Cecily cried out.

Splash.

Splash?

I bent over the hole, but Dad held me back. "Time to go."

FLOYD ROBINETT
Thorne

Thirty minutes later, we sat in a hotel flat Mortimer had spontaneously booked.

I knew I would never forget how he had led us back through the tunnel labyrinth and then just left us at some crossing, only to return with his wife in his arms a few minutes later. She was shaking heavily. In the entire past year, I had never seen Nevada Morrigane *this* broken.

Mortimer had carried her the whole way to the car, then had driven into the city. It was risky, of course, but apparently, he hadn't seen any other way.

And well, it was the best solution, given what was on the news when we arrived.

The war is starting. See you in White Lilies Creek.

The Eternals had – for the first time ever – reached out to the media to send this letter.

What it meant? Nobody knew.

We would find out the next day.

What had happened in the catacombs?

Nevada said when Mortimer had shot Cecily's hand, she'd stumbled back in pain and fell through one of the tunnels right into the lagoon. It was likely she'd survived.

"Good," Sparrow mumbled. "After all, nobody deserves to die, right?"

Nevada shook her head. "Sparrow, Birdie, I have kept you in a safe bubble, away from death and murder, for your whole life, but I'm starting to believe it was a mistake. We are at war. I agree that death is a terrible thing, and murder even more so, but we need to put an end to the Eternal Magicians' cruelty. The only way to do so is to kill them."

"But you can't kill them with mortal weapons," I added. "As I said, there's that spell in the grimoire–"

"Isn't it ironic that they have a spell in their own grimoire that gets them killed?" Sparrow asked.

"Well…" I shrugged. "It kills all Eternals that are in a certain radius around the person saying the spell – except, of course, for the one who says it. So if they wanted to get rid of somebody from another family – or even their own…" I didn't speak on. My cousin Lilith.

"So you're absolutely sure that this grimoire exists and will help us?" Nemo dug deeper.

"Absolutely." I nodded reluctantly. "There's just the reason I lied and said I don't know where it was at first – I'm not sure if it will kill me as well. I could still have some of the blood in me, from the last rite I attended. But… it used to be in their library, I think. Clarisse used to collect black magic spells and potions in it." I tried to recall some memories about that book, but it'd been some years since I'd last seen it. Once, I had stood next to her as she wrote down a deadly spell…

"*Grandmother,*" I heard little Thorne – little Phoenix Kyril LeDoux – ask. "*What are you doing?*"

She had closed the book immediately, but I'd caught some of the clean, ornate words already. Death, blood, rite. The usual.

The cover of the book... "It's made of leather," I said. "Brown and black." The image on my mind blurred and the harder I tried to recall it, the more it faded. "Red, too."

That's the thing about memories. The more you want to remember, the faster they vanish until you aren't even able to say if they were real, or were a dream once.

"Perfect." Nevada gave me a grave look. "I am not sure how this war will turn out, but we need to get that grimoire in any case."

"That's for sure," Mortimer added. "The army will be here in a few hours. I am not sure if we have any chance to get to the manor then, when fighters are everywhere."

He handed his tablet over to us.

Eternal Magicians took over entire school.

The headline of an online newspaper.

I skimmed through the article. Apparently, a magical boarding school in southern England had been attacked by a group of students and teachers during dinner in the great hall, where they had threatened the others with guns and knives, claiming to kill everybody who wouldn't obey. Since nobody had resisted, nobody had gotten hurt either, but it was incredibly scary to see what the Eternals were capable of.

"How did they get *students* on their side? *Children*?" Jasmine whispered.

"Maybe with the temptation of becoming immortal? Maybe they promised them power, or stronger magic powers with some alchemical spells?" I shrugged. "It doesn't surprise me too much. They have their ways."

"But after all that was on the news last year?" Nevada shook her head. "I'm not sure if reasonable magically gifted people would join a group of cruel killers, just for a bit of power. I'd rather suspect they used magic to influence them. Some mind-controlling potion? I don't know."

"They could have just given that to everybody then. Why that attack in the dinner hall? They could have worked on their plan in secret!" Jasmine asked.

"I don't think anything was ever about being secretive." Mortimer laughed. "I don't know much about them – luckily – but from what Nevada has told me and from what was in the media, I am sure they are aware of the aftermath of that attack. Fame."

"It doesn't matter. It happened as it did, and we can't change anything about it." Nevada got up, her hands still shaking a bit as she collected our empty tea cups. "For now, it's time to sleep. Tomorrow is gonna be… messy."

Messy.

That was probably the right word to describe whatever she was planning. She was either going to talk to the army leaders or avoid them as she'd fight alongside her police colleagues.

"Time to sleep?" Sparrow let out a bitter laugh. "Are you sure you don't mean *send the kids to bed and then stay up all night to make plans?*"

"I meant it the way I said it." Nevada gave her a grave look. I had never seen her as exhausted as now, but it was fair. After all, Cecily Williams had tried to kill her.

❧ 🕷 ☙

Sparrow

I woke up to the sound of gunshots.
"Thorne, turn down that fucking video game, it's only five AM-"
I sat up straight. Yes, it was 5AM, but Thorne had never in his life played a single shooter game. There was only one possibility.

The war had begun.

I quickly put on some clothes and went to the kitchen, where the others were standing by the window.

"... no way this can take a good turn," Mum said. "They are too weak. Good morning, Sparrow."

Everybody turned to me.

"It's happening," Dad said, as if I hadn't realised that myself. "The army arrived two hours ago~"

"~and has had to give up two districts already." Mum shrugged. "This is a senseless war."

"What do they even want to do with White Lilies Creek once they've defeated the army?" I asked, a bit surprised by her careless voice.

"Power." She sighed. "I'm afraid they are planning to take over the fucking country. The entire fucking damned country of England."

"The whole fucking damned country of England?" I repeated slowly. "But how~ why~"

"They're insane, we've talked about this already."

"But~"

"And they are dangerous. The problem is that we have two units of enemies. On the one hand the Eternals, who are immortal but don't have any magical powers – just some alchemical potions, and mortal weapons. On the other hand, the Wickeds fighting by their side. They aren't immortal, but have strong magical powers that protect them. And since there's no way to determine who you are battling at that very moment..." She didn't speak on.

"And what do you want to do now?" Thorne asked.

"There's just one thing I can think of right now." She didn't have to speak on. The graveness of her voice and the tired look in her eyes said it all.

"You want to talk to the army leader," I said.

She moved her head to a slight nod.

"He might kill you."

"Or he might accept that he could need me." She turned on the coffee machine. "We know things that they don't know."

"That's blackmailing," Jasmine mumbled.

"That's my life insurance," Mum shot back in a sharp voice.

"So what *are* the things we know that they don't know?" Thorne asked. "I thought you'd given the media all information we have."

"The teens and teachers who attacked the school in the south," Mum said and sat down on a chair with her coffee. "What do you think, what made them become Wickeds?"

"We talked about that last night already, didn't we?" Thorne said impatiently. "Either mental influence or magical influence."

"And *who* influenced them?" Mum dug deeper, and I understood.

"You mean the resurrected teens? The ones that were~" My voice broke in excitement. "Those who were sent to magical boarding schools all over the country two weeks ago..."

"Correct." Mum sighed. "Nobody knows the resurrection happened for *that* reason. So that's something we know that the army doesn't. And there's also the grimoire."

"We should split up," Dad suggested. "You go to the army leader, and I go into the manor."

"No way!" Mum and I said simultaneously.

"No?" Dad frowned.

"You're coming with me. The kids are going into the manor to look for the grimoire," Mum said. "They know the place much better than you, and it will keep them from doing dangerous, uncontrolled things."

I wanted to protest, but she was right. If she'd force us to stay here, we were most likely to go out and try to help on our own.

"I will call the army leader now." She took a deep breath. "And you can listen, so you understand what kind of situation I'm in."

She took out her phone and dialled a number, then put it on loudspeaker so we could all hear along.

Somebody picked up, followed by a long silence.

"Nevada Morrigane," a male voice eventually said, oddly calm. "Who else could it be, calling me after causing a catastrophe?"

"Floyd Robinett. Who else could it be, hiding his own failure from the whole world?" Mum gave back.

"You haven't changed at all, Morrigane. Not at all." He didn't sound surprised and his voice was almost soft.

"I was told the same thing yesterday, by Cecily Williams. Who tried to kill me."

Silence again.

"She should've succeeded, don't you agree?" There was amusement in the man's voice.

"You haven't changed either, Floyd." Mum sounded just as amused. "I'm surprised your assassins haven't found me yet."

"Oh, we know where you are. White Lilies Creek, Creek Hotel 18 Theatre Road, third floor. Sitting at the table with a cup of coffee."

Mum froze for a second, then she straightened her back. "How many?"

"Snipers? A bunch." Robinett chuckled. "You didn't call for nothing, correct?"

"Have I ever called for nothing?"

"No. Speak now. So we can finish this quickly."

"I know things you don't know. Things that could change the situation out there."

"Things you're keeping from us to assure we'll let you live. What if we killed you before you can tell us?"

"You'd be just as selfish as I am, putting the outcome of the war on a knife-edge."

"Glad we agree." The man laughed. "I can't believe you've managed to once again get us under your control. You're playing with us, even after you owe the army your life."

Mum just shrugged. "So we have a deal?"

"A deal?" He laughed again. "I know better than to make deals with you. We have an open agreement that stays valid until the war is over. After that, you will get an army trial."

Mum flinched, but didn't let him realise anything. "Alright. Let's meet in half an hour outside the city."

"You're insane, Morrigane." He laughed again. "How did you know I'm in White Lilies Creek as well?"

Mum raised her hand with her pistol and pointed it towards the window without even looking there. "Is that an answer enough, Floyd?"

"See you in half an hour."

Click.

"Wow." Mum lowered the phone and ran her hands through her hair. "Insane. Everything's insane."

"What does all that mean?" Jasmine asked.

"I'm safe. For now." Mum sighed. "Until the war is over. And I will go and give all information to him."

"What... what exactly is your connection to him?" I carefully dug deeper. "That didn't sound like he's just your ex-boss. And why do you owe the army your life?"

"Oh, long story." Mum shook her head. "I need to hurry now."

"And what are *we* gonna do?"

"Change of plans." She got up. "I'm going alone, and you will stay here until I return. Maybe Floyd will give me some news in return, too. Stay inside, don't open the door for anyone, always keep your weapons within reach. And if I don't return, run. Save your ass. If Floyd thinks it's a good idea to even kill me during the war, he's lost his mind."

🕷

Jasmine

"Any good plans about what we are going to do now?"

"Stay inside, don't open the door for anyone, and keep our weapons within reach." Sparrow gave me a serious look. "Jasmine, I know you've been dead before, and that might have been pretty relaxing, but I really don't know how to resurrect you if you'd happen to die again."

I flinched. "That's not funny."

The corners of Sparrow's mouth twitched as she tried to stay calm. "Jasmine! I am *dead* serious!"

Thorne giggled and now neither Sparrow nor I could hold back the laughter.

For a few minutes, we just stood in the kitchen laughing.

Until Mr. Morrigane raised his finger to his lips. "Did you hear that too?"

"What...?" I asked, but Sparrow nodded. "Someone's at the door!"

"What, really?" A cold flash of fear shot through my body.

"Someone knocked," Mr. Morrigane said.

We stood in silence for a moment, and there it was again. It wasn't a knock, more like... like someone was trying to pry the door open!

Before I knew what I was doing, I had a gun in my hands. Sparrow, Thorne and Sparrow's dad grabbed weapons as well, and then we exchanged insecure looks.

"This doesn't seem like the right moment to confess that unlike Nemo, I have never killed anyone, right?" Mr. Morrigane gave us an unhappy grin.

"What?" Sparrow stared at him, her voice pitching. "Mum left us here and none of us are able to kill?"

"Correct. I swear I tried, but I even failed to kill Cecily." He cleared his throat. "I'm nothing like Nevada."

So we were helpless. None of us teens were able to kill. Sparrow herself was the only one who could properly use a gun. I mean, her mother had tried to teach Thorne and me and it wasn't too complicated, but the situation stressed me out and I had always been bad at aiming.

So we just stood there in the kitchen, exchanging helpless looks, until Sparrow shook her head and made a move. "This has to end."

She walked straight outside into the hallway and to the door, lifted the gun and said in the clearest, mimicked voice of her mother, "This is Nemo Morrigane. If you aren't gonna leave in a second, I'm gonna shoot you through the door. All of you. Before you can even count to three. If you are even able to count, stupid idiots."

The noise stopped. Voices whispered.

"One," Sparrow said.

"Prove it, Nemo!" someone called.

"Two."

Silence. And then, muffled steps on the carpeted floor. Away from us.

"Amazing." Sparrow walked right past Thorne and me, dropped in a chair and grabbed the coffee pot from the table. "Time for a strong cup of coffee."

"What..." I cleared my throat. "Where did you learn that?"

"Mum taught me." Sparrow put the can back and wrapped her fingers around the warm cup. The smell of hot coffee spread through the apartment. "She taught me some things that she learned in the army herself. Some when I was younger, and some just now in preparation for the war."

"That's amazing," Thorne said. "I think you just saved us."

"I think so too." A relieved smile appeared on Sparrow's lips as she confessed, "I didn't think it would actually work!"

"Even I almost thought it was Nemo," Mr. Morrigane confessed with a grin. "You're incredible, Sparrow."

LIFE AND DEATH
Sparrow

Half an hour later, Mum returned, bloodstains on her clothes.

She dropped down on the couch and closed her eyes without a single word. Thorne and Jasmine stayed in the hallway to lock and block the door again, but I followed Mum and Dad into the living room.

"What happened?" Dad immediately sat down next to her and removed a bloody strand of hair from her face to reveal a cut along her jaw. "Did *he* do that?"

"I wish it was that easy." Mum sighed. "We got attacked and he saved my life."

"But only so he–?"

Mum nodded. "Only so he can hold that trial after the war. With himself as the judge."

I didn't understand anything anymore. If that guy was serious, he had an incredible joy torturing Mum like this.

"And how did the conversation go?" Jasmine and Thorne joined us.

"Horrible." Mum sighed. "It was a trap. And I walked right into it. Mort – we are back in the army."

"Seriously?" Dad flinched.

"Seriously. He had two snipers. If I hadn't agreed... This was a deal breaker!" She threw a handkerchief against the wall. "I should have known he's not to trust!"

"This is either a twisted way of saying how good and important you were back then..." I slowly said. "Or an attempt at revenge. Risking your life and all."

"Or both." Mum sighed. "He can't accept that his best fighter chose to betray him."

"And so you're gonna join them?" Thorne asked.

"We don't have another choice." She sighed. "He will kill us instantly if we resist. God beware what he'd do if he knew I'm keeping the information on the grimoire from him."

"But he will find out after the war!" Thorne said. "I mean, if we use the grimoire to kill the LeDouxes..."

"After the war, everything is lost anyway." Mum gave him a melancholic smile.

"Has the army ever used torture?" Jasmine asked, then quickly added, "Not that I think you'd deserve it. Just-just in general."

Mum gave her a tired smile. "*The army*, as you put it, has of course used torture. Imagine every human right you can think of. We've broken all of them. Those were the magic wars, Jasmine. Of course the army used torture. Of course I used torture."

She kept silent and I felt cold all of a sudden. How could she handle it that calmly?

"And is torture still… practised today?" Jasmine carefully inquired.

"I know what you're implying. Don't worry, they're not gonna harm you or Thorne."

How reassuring, so I would only lose my mother in the trial. Or Dad? Would they harm Dad, other than by putting him back into the army? She hadn't said anything about him or~ I frowned. "Hold the fuck up, Mum…"

She looked away.

"*Mum?*"

"I can't promise anything, Birdie." She turned to me and gave me a grave look. "They already got Mortimer involved, so what tells me they're not gonna harm you? And they don't even know yet you were there with me."

I felt dizzy. "They're gonna… torture me?"

"I don't know." She shook her head and buried it in her hands. "I don't know anything. I feel like I'm caught in a nightmare."

They might torture me. I couldn't wrap my head around it. It felt too unreal. I had escaped from White Lilies Manor a year ago, and again two weeks ago, only to now possibly die at the hands of the army? No way this was for real.

"The only good news I have," Mum said slowly, "is that I stole the list with the resurrected teens and the places they've been sent to."

"The list with the teens?" Thorne frowned. "Where did you get that?"

Mum smiled shortly. "When Floyd and I started talking, he immediately sent some people to the Manor. One of them had super vision and could read the list through a window. And before I left, I made sure to steal the list." She pulled a wrinkled sheet out of her pocket. "Here you go." She handed it to Thorne. "Maybe you remember some of them."

"Unlikely. Jasmine said most of them were Victorian," Thorne said, but looked at the handwritten list for a moment. Then, he dropped it.

"I'll be back in a second," he said mindlessly and left, but he hadn't turned his face fast enough to hide he'd turned pale.

I picked up the list.

And I can only assume I turned just as pale as Thorne the second I saw the name on top of the list.

Thorne

"Thorne?" Sparrow entered our bedroom. "Are you okay?"

I turned around and wiped the tears from my face, but it was in vain.

Sparrow dropped on the bed beside me. "I've seen it. The name. Everest Beckett. And I just wanted to know if I can... help you. Help you to meet him or to avoid him, depending on what you want."

"Bold of you to assume I know what I want." My voice was weak, but I tried to smile.

"I just thought..." She gave me an insecure look. "Why are you crying?"

"I don't know." I sighed. "It's all too much right now. And if that's what you want to know... yes, we argued back then. We argued, and we never had a chance to say sorry. I tried to send him away, but he didn't believe me because I didn't give any certain details as I feared Rosary finding out about it."

"Finding out about your relationship or finding out about that you've told him about the rite?"

"Both, to be honest." I closed my eyes to recall the image of my first love. His shoulder length blond hair, his green eyes, the way his lips moved when he smiled. How he scratched his nose when he was nervous.

"Wanna talk about your time together?" Sparrow asked, but I sensed that she was just as uncomfortable as I was. It was just weird to talk about my ex with my current girlfriend.

"No, it's okay. Let's go back." I touched her hand and forced a weak smile onto my lips, and she nodded. "You... know that you can talk to my family about it if you want to, right? They're the most supportive people I know. My mum knows about it anyway because she was there when you came out to the LeDouxes, and my dad will support you too. Just in case you'd want them to know, so that they don't accidentally hurt him or whatever..." She seemed insecure, and I could understand. She didn't know Everest. She was wondering if he was a part of the Eternals now, if he had believed the LeDouxes just as Jasmine had. And to be honest, I was wondering the same.

⤳ 🕷 ⤶

Sparrow

"Floyd has already sent fighters to the schools," Mum said when we returned. "But I'm afraid it's too late. The Wickeds will attack as soon as they sense the army members coming."

"Why are they waiting anyway?" Jasmine asked, but answered for herself in the same moment, "It's a power play, right? Every time we think we're safe, they attack another school."

"Exactly." Mum sighed. "There are twelve schools. Three of them have already been attacked today."

"So what's the plan now?" Thorne asked in a hoarse voice.

"Mortimer and I are going to support the army. And you..." She hesitated. "Let's talk again tonight. I want to have a look at how good the Manor is guarded."

"We're supposed to stay here alone?" Jasmine stared at her. "Mrs. Morrigane, we almost got attacked already!"

"Sorry?" Mum frowned and Jasmine summed up what had happened.

"They're insane." Mum shook her head. "But I won't let you go to the Manor already. Not before I know how many people are there."

"So?"

"Let's do something unexpected." Mum hesitated. "You go get the groceries."

"Please *what?*" Jasmine stared at her.

"I'm serious. They don't expect you in stores. And... we need food anyway. We can't risk eating down in the hotel dining hall because someone could poison your– *our* food too easily. You have to go. Please take your weapons, though."

"Are any stores even open?" Thorne asked.

"Sure. Just because there's war doesn't mean people don't need food. You are not safe here alone anymore and neither the army nor the Wickeds will expect you out there." Mum sighed. "End of the discussion. We leave after lunch."

TRICKED
Sparrow

We left the flat through the stairway of the Victorian hotel. Was anybody watching us from the lobby? I shivered and hurried outside along with the others. Mum and Dad had left a few minutes ago without much ado – they must be going through hell right now.

"Where are we going?" Thorne inquired.

Jasmine pointed vaguely into a direction. "Nemo said shops are open in the southern quarters because the fights are currently happening in the centre of the city. You know, with the army coming from the South and the Eternals and Wickeds coming from the North, from the manor."

"And right now, we are…?" I asked.

"A bit north of the city centre." Thorne gave me a worried look. "We should avoid getting closer. How about a walk through the nature surrounding White Lilies Creek?"

And so we went, Thorne leading us, through narrow lanes and towards the outskirts of the city. Nobody was to be seen, just the occasional car. Even the paths in the fields were lonely – places where under normal circumstances, dozens of people would've gone for a walk in this sunny weather.

Normal circumstances.

We reached the southern part of the city without problems and went from store to store, filled bag after bag, paid bills after bills. Three, maybe four hours later we made our way back to the hotel, again through the fields.

We walked in silence. What was there to say, anyway?

A black car passed us by. Oddly slow. And stopped.

"Run!" I screamed and we hasted across the meadow, but it was too late. A man in a long coat had already left the car and grabbed my arm with incredible speed.

I screamed and kicked as he pulled me back onto the street, but it was in vain. He was too strong.

From the corner of my eye, I caught a glimpse of Thorne and Jasmine standing in the meadow, frozen like statues. What was happening here?

I tried to kick and hit the man, struggling to break free. Bones met bones, but his grip was too tight. He slammed my forehead against the edge of the car's door, and I sank to my knees.

"They told me you'd be aggressive, but nobody warned me it'd be *this* bad!" The man laughed. "And after all, I'm here for peace!"

I knew that voice from somewhere.

And wasn't his red-black coat part of the army's uniform?

This could only mean one thing.

"You can tell those lies to your mother!" I hissed and tried to get up again, but he continued to push me to the ground.

"Or to *your* mother – if you know who I am?" He laughed again.

"'Course I do. Floyd Robinett, army leader asshole," I gave back through clenched teeth.

"Almost." He twisted my arms behind my back and I suppressed a scream. "Sir Floyd Richard Robinett, if you please."

"Oh, how could I forget that?" I let out a sarcastic laugh, then tried to turn my head to catch a glimpse of his face. That face I'd seen years ago in a history book about the wars, along with Mum's.

But he didn't allow my movement.

"I've got news from your mother," he just said.

Don't say– don't say she's–

My resistance broke for a moment and he pulled me off the ground to press me against the closed back door of the car.

"She told me something that I need to fact-check."

So she's alive.

"And that is?" I stared at the tinted glass, past my mirrored self. Still no chance of seeing him: the long hood threw dark shadows on his face. And Thorne and Jasmine still stood in that meadow like statues.

"That she wasn't the one who committed the crime."

"The crime?"

"You don't need to play stupid. No chance of making me believe that. You're your mother's child, after all."

"I'll take that as a compliment."

"Maybe it was one."

"But I thought you hated my mother?"

"I still know what she was worth to me and the army. Before she betrayed me." His voice had become full of hate. "But what do you even know about her? You know nothing, little Morrigane, nothing!"

"What- what do you mean?" Was he bluffing or was there actually something Mum was keeping from us?

"Oh, forget it. I ain't gonna be the one to destroy your family."

"You- you're joking."

"Maybe." He kept silent for a moment, before his grip tightened again. "And now tell me the truth. Your mother said you broke into Headquarters in her place." He let go of my wrists and grabbed my shoulders, forcing me to turn around so I could finally see his face. "It was *you*, wasn't it?"

He still looked the same as in that old history book. For a moment, I forgot his question. Just stared at him. He didn't look like a murderer at all, and yet he very much did. Wasn't he just a normal man of maybe forty years? But behind the wrinkles and scars, his lively dark eyes, half covered by strands of black hair, reminded me who he really was. The leader of the army. A mass murderer.

So this was the man who wanted to kill my mother.

"The truth, Morrigane. Tell me the truth."

"It's wrong. I wasn't at Headquarters." Mum had kept my name out of the media for a reason, so I stuck with this lie for now. But why had she told him I'd been there *without her*? Did she want to confuse him?

"We found your fingerprints." His fingernails pierced my skin. "I can sense lies, that's my magic power. And I think by now you realised I despise liars."

"Aren't you a liar yourself?" I gave back and cursed my tongue in the same moment.

"Maybe I despise myself."

His change between personal, sarcastic honesty and literal death threats confused me and I honestly wasn't sure what to think of him. On one hand he gave me the impression of a 2000s emo teen, and on the other hand he was the cruel leader of the magic army.

"We were both there. She brought me along," I finally confessed.

Robinett took a step back and nodded with a grin. "That's all I wanted to know. Your mum and I are really looking forward to your trial."

I understood.

With knees like pudding, I leant against the car. He'd fooled me, of course he had. Mum had not told him about me breaking into Headquarters on my own, nor had anybody found my fingerprints. He'd simply had an assumption, had bluffed, and I'd been stupid enough to fall for the trick.

"We'll meet after the war." He smiled. "And don't try to escape. You'll only make it worse."

"Why?" I whispered. "Aren't you supposed to protect us?"

His expression turned harsh. "Your mother and you, you are traitors. You don't deserve protection."

The door of the car fell shut, the engine roared and I fell to my knees as the car drove off.

Thorne pulled me into his arms a second later, and Jasmine joined us, shaking her limbs.

"Sparrow, are you all right?" Thorne whispered.

"Assume so. You?"

"What the heck was that?" Jasmine shook her head. "I felt like I was frozen in my movement! Like a statue!"

Thorne let out a deep sigh. "This Robinett is a strong enemy. The freezing trick, and sensing lies –

these are two very strong powers. And he has the whole army under his control!"

☙ 🕷 ❧

Jasmine

Dark clouds covered the sky as we silently made our way back home. The incident with the army leader had left us all shocked and surprised, even though it was exactly what Nemo had announced would happen.

So Sparrow was going to be on trial too.

Would she actually die or be tortured?

Her mother hadn't denied the possibility, but could that man really be *that* cruel? Was he really able to kill a child?

Sparrow was giving her best to not make us realise her concern, but it was obvious she was scared. How could she not?

We reached the hotel through a narrow lane.

"There's a light on in the kitchen," Thorne slowly said. "We didn't leave it on, did we?"

Sparrow frowned. "Most certainly not."

"Your parents?" I asked.

"I doubt they're back already," she said with insecurity in her voice. "It's not even 6pm."

"So?" Thorne slowly said. "Are we gonna go inside?"

"Do we have a choice?" she replied as lightning flashed across the sky. "We could either stay out here and get soaked in the rain that's coming towards us, or..."

"Or go in and die?" I frowned.

"Exactly." Sparrow gave me a quick smile. "Let's go in."

HIS RETURN
Jasmine

The hotel lobby was empty.

We snuck upstairs, glancing around every corner before walking on, until we reached the door to our flat.

Yeah, something was wrong here.

The door was damaged around the lock, as if someone had tried to open it with an axe.

"Is this new?" Sparrow whispered. "Or is that from this morning?"

"No clue." Thorne frowned. "It could be new. When your Mum returned, she didn't say anything. And she definitely used the door."

"So it's new?" I felt dizzy. "Is someone inside?"

"I assume so." Sparrow had an odd calmness in her voice as she took out her gun. "Could be time for our first murder, right?"

"Are you insane?" My voice broke.

"Not directly. I just don't want to die." She shrugged as if she didn't care.

But of course, she was scared.

She pushed against the door, then paused. "It won't move."

"What does that mean?" I asked. "Is it blocked?"

"Not blocked." She hesitated. "Locked."

"Locked? That means nobody actually broke in?" Thorne frowned. "Or they had the key..."

"Or magical lock-opening powers." I pushed up my sleeves and motioned for Sparrow to step aside, then I pulled a hairpin from my hair. Two seconds later, the mechanism clicked.

"I'll go first," Sparrow hissed and kicked it open.

Sparrow

The door slammed against the wall and if anyone was in there, they must have heard us by now.

I raised the gun and made my way through the short hallway towards the kitchen. Thorne and Jasmine followed me, their own weapons raised.

One more step towards the kitchen. The door was ajar and I carefully pushed it open.

It all happened within seconds. Someone reached out from behind the door and grabbed my gun, ripped it out of my hands, almost broke my trigger finger in the process and then, I was lying on the ground.

My back ached, and the fact that somebody suddenly knelt on it made it no better. The worst, however, was probably the barrel of my own gun that was being pressed to the back of my head. I wanted to scream, to jump up, to attack whoever was there, but I didn't even dare to breathe. This had to be one of the Wickeds, since the army was waiting to kill me until the war was over.

"Let my girlfriend go or I'll kill you!" Thorne yelled, but the person ignored him entirely.

"What are you doing here, intruders?" a voice hissed into my ear. A *young* voice.

"This is our hotel room that we paid for, unlike you!" I replied through clenched teeth. This was the second attack for today and I was slowly getting too weak and exhausted to fight.

"Now drop that damned weapon and get up— What the heck are *you* doing here?" Thorne's voice broke. "*You*, out of all people?"

The pressure on my back lessened and as I raised my head, the person was now kneeling next to me, staring at Thorne with wide green eyes. "Phoenix?"

⤇ 🕷 ⤆

Thorne

Out of all people.

Out of all people, Everest Beckett had broken into our flat and threatened Sparrow. It was so ironic. Out of all people, him.

"Phoenix?" he repeated and got up, throwing the gun onto the counter.

I cleared my throat. "Thorne. I go by Thorne now."

Wow, I was reunited with my dead lover and all I could do was tell him my new name.

I had dreamt of this moment so often, how we would meet and everything would be like back then, when we had been happy together. But nothing was like back then. We were strangers now, practically. He used to be the older one, the one I looked up to, and now I was the older one. I was also in a relationship with Sparrow now. And we still didn't know~

"What the heck are you doing here?" I asked for the third time.

"Hey, I know you!" Jasmine threw in. "You were in the circle! Everest, right? *Wait* – are you *that* boy?"

"Good afternoon, Jasmine." Everest just smiled and bowed down.

My heart skipped a beat. Okay, he had not changed at all.

"I solemnly apologize for the way I treated you." He turned to Sparrow and helped her up, but she just stared at me. It was easy to see what she was thinking about. Whether I would leave her for him.

"I think there's a lot I have to explain." He ran his hand through his hand and smiled at me again. "Let's sit down."

I nodded quietly and led him to the living room, where he sat down to my right on the sofa. Sparrow sat down to my left. Jasmine took her seat in the armchair, probably already figuring out the same thing as Sparrow.

It scared me, honestly. I loved Sparrow with my whole heart, but I used to love Everest in the same way. *Used to.*

All I hoped for now was that I wouldn't ever catch feelings for him again.

"So, I woke up in that stone circle with all the other teens," he said. "Like all of them, I knew nothing about my previous life and my previous love." He wiggled his eyebrows.

"Uh, about that~" I cleared my throat and pointed to Sparrow.

"That's fair." He shrugged, but he looked a bit hurt. "I mean, if I had listened to you~ if we had run away together..."

"Continue your story," Jasmine demanded.

"Alright. So, I obeyed the LeDouxes at first, but just this afternoon, while I was roaming through the library, I found two books that changed my view. One dealt with the assignments each of the teens had to fulfil after their resurrection, and one... was a personal story. A diary. As I read both of them, all my memories returned."

A diary. Yeah, *my* diary. I'd put it in the library to leave behind all the memories when I changed my identity and fled from the Manor.

"I wanted to know what this meant, how I ended up on the wrong side of this war, and I hoped you as their main enemies could maybe tell me some things. So out on the streets, I found a bunch of Wickeds that led me straight to this flat. They wanted to pry open the door, but I hypnotized them to stop. So I opened the door with my second magic powers, went inside and locked it again. And waited for you."

"And attacked us," Sparrow said in a cold voice.

"I'm sorry. I thought you were intruders. You see, I didn't quite expect teens. Rather adult fighters like Nemo."

"She's my mother," Sparrow said dryly.

"Congrats." He sounded genuinely impressed. Then, he grinned. "So, Phoenix – Thorne – what did I miss in the past five years?"

Five years. It had only been five years, but it felt like so much longer.

"After your death–" My voice broke. "I did what I wanted to do together with you. I faked my death and fled. And two years ago, I returned and applied for a room. Last Summer Solstice night, together with Sparrow and Jasmine, I tried to fight the LeDouxes."

"I died," Jasmine added dryly.

"And the whole thing about the Arcane Wars that are restarting? Is that related?"

"Obviously. That's why they brought back a bunch of you. They want revenge." I hesitated. "And they've got the Wickeds on their side. They want revenge for what the army did to them. The army was wrong."

"Sorry?" He stared at me, scrunching up his nose in disbelief. "The army was wrong killing them?"

"Yep. Because Thill LeDoux gave them wrong information on purpose."

"You're living quite the adventurous life." He grinned.

"Adventurous?" Sparrow shook her head. "We are risking our life on a daily base."

Slam.

The door collided with the wall. Sparrow jumped up, grabbed a gun from the table and stormed into the hallway, but it was just Nevada and Mortimer who returned from their mission.

"Who the fuck damaged our door?" Nevada was furious. "You all better be safe and healthy! And who the fuck is on our sofa?"

Everest got up and bowed again. "Everest Beckett. I assume I am talking to famous assassin Nevada Nemo Morrigane?"

Nevada calmed down immediately and gave me a short smile, before nodding and turning back to him.

"Exactly. Nice to meet you, Everest. What brings you here?"

"I am on your side, if that's what you wanna hear." He sat back down. "I know everything that's going on right now. Is there any way I can support you?"

Nevada and Mortimer exchanged a look and only now, I saw both of them were injured. Nevada had a bleeding wound on her cheek and Mortimer was limping.

"I trust you. We wouldn't be alive anymore if you wanted us dead." Mum sighed. "But do the LeDouxes know you're on our side?"

"No, Mrs. Morrigane. They think I'm currently on a mission."

"Then could you bring us their grimoire, maybe?" she suggested.

Genius idea. None of us would have to return to the Manor if that worked out!

"The grimoire?" He raised his eyebrows. "Sure. If you tell me what that is."

"Thorne?" Nevada gave me a prompting look and I described the book to him.

"And the serum," she then added. "Everest – do you know anything about the serum or whatever they use to turn everybody at the schools into Wickeds?"

"Oh, that's not a serum. It's hypnosis powers! They only resurrected teens that have hypnosis powers!"

"I don't." Jasmine frowned.

"But you were a good way to confuse us and bring us back to the Manor," Sparrow said with a shrug. "They really planned everything out."

"Of course they did." Nevada rubbed her temples. "Please just tell me that your shopping tour went without problems."

The three of us just stared at each other.

Nevada sighed. "Do I wanna know?"

⁊ 🕷 ⳺

"**T**hat asshole, that incredibly cruel asshole!" Nevada Morrigane walked up and down the living room, cursing and swearing about Floyd Robinett. "I can't believe he's even attacking *children* now! Are you injured, Sparrow? I'm gonna sue him, I'm gonna put him right back into a trial, I'm gonna kill him personally, I want to see him suffer~"

"Calm down, Mum." Sparrow sounded tired. "Let's not think about him for now. Let's make dinner and plan what we're going to do next."

"Alright." Nevada let out a deep sigh. "Off to the kitchen, then. All of you."

I got up to follow the others, but Everest held me back. "I made a mistake."

"That is?"

He gave me a grave look. "I can't tell you yet. I know you'll find out, but I can't say it now. I just– I am sorry. Tell everybody I'm sorry once you've found out."

"What the heck is going on? I thought I could trust you!"

"You can trust me. Just – whatever is going to happen, don't worry about me. Please." He smiled again, got up and went to the kitchen.

I followed him.

Looking back on it – it was idiotic of me to not dig deeper, but on the other hand, nothing could have changed the outcome anymore. What was done was done.

OLD FRIENDSHIPS
Sparrow

Mum forced me to help her clean the dishes, and I knew she didn't actually need the help. She called me into the kitchen to talk.

"So, what's up?" I said and grabbed a towel.

She plunged her hands with the plates into the hot water. "Are you okay?"

"What do you mean? We're at war, Mum."

She sighed. "I mean because of what happened today."

"That I met Robinett?"

"What else could I be talking about?" She handed me the plate a bit more forcefully than necessary. "Sparrow, I am worried about you. Meeting Floyd Robinett doesn't just pass one by like a light breeze!"

"He didn't hurt me too much." I hesitated, put the dry plate into the closet. "Except for when he slammed my head against the car. Okay, yeah, maybe he did hurt me. But not too badly."

"Not too badly?" Mum spun around and water splashed everywhere. "He shouldn't have even *touched* you in the first place!" Water soaked my shirt as she placed her wet palms on my shoulders. "I want to know what else he did. Tell me everything. So that I can make him pay when I meet him the next time."

She was ready to kill. The realisation struck me like lightning. Mum would kill for me. It was more than anything anyone had ever done for me, but I wasn't sure if I really wanted it. She would only make it all worse for us, wouldn't she? The trial – she would be charged with murder. With *real* murder. Not just with war crimes, not just with being a traitor.

"Don't try to protect him, Sparrow, he doesn't deserve your mercy. Every little mistake, every little thing he did. It only adds up to his pile of sins. He has crossed a line today."

"His pile of sins?" I frowned. "You still haven't told me about what connects you and him. It's not just that he was your boss, right? There's more."

She turned away, back to the sink, and chucked one innocent fork after the other into the water. A minute of silence passed.

"Mum?" I tapped her shoulder. "Please tell me."

"I'm ashamed," Mum gave back in a bitter tone. "If I hadn't taken it all that far, he'd be a different person by now. Maybe."

"Sorry?"

She took a deep breath and focused on scrubbing an imaginary stain off a fork.

"Mum..."

"Yeah." She pulled the plug and the water went down the drain with a hollow groan. "I'll tell you."

"Please." I pulled myself up onto the kitchen counter and she perched beside me, like we had done so often since I had been a toddler, every time we talked about something serious.

"I lied to you. Remember when Floyd said I owe the army my life?"

I nodded slowly.

"I didn't run away from home at the age of 15 to join the army, or whatever silly story I told you. I said I don't know where my parents are today. But I know. They are dead. I am an orphan. And my parents were *Eternals.*" Her voice broke and I stared at her. Mum was the daughter of people like the LeDouxes? *And I was the granddaughter of people like the LeDouxes.* A feeling of cold shock hit me.

"The army killed them in a battle. I never got to know the exact context and I never really cared, either. Long story short, they could have killed me as well. It would have been legal. I could have posed a threat to the country in the future, if I'd grow up and have the evilness in my genes or whatever. But they decided to let me live, as I was only barely a year old. And they put me in an orphanage run by the army, educated me and the other kids there from the very beginning that the army were the good guys, and with 12 I got to join the fighting programme." Her voice broke. "I'm nothing like my parents."

"I know." I could hardly form a smile. "Is that why you and Thorne get along so well?"

"Maybe." She shook her head. "Sparrow... nobody knows about this. Except for the few people in the army who decided to give me to the orphanage, Mortimer, you, and Floyd."

"Robinett? Why did you tell them?"

"We used to be something like... friends." Tears hung on the tips of her lashes. "He's ten years older than me. When I joined the army in 1999, he had just gotten a higher rank. Not the army leader, but the leader of the department – the training unit – that I joined. And as I said, I was twelve and the army was my biggest dream. I was enthusiastic, maybe the most enthusiastic of all newbies, and he picked me to become his personal student. He was my mentor for the following – yeah, four years. Up to early 2003. He became the army leader, and two months later, the war started." She sighed. "But not only the Arcane Magic Wars. Also our very personal war. Our connection had gotten intense, but I'm not sure if it was in a good or bad way. You know how they often say the student exceeds the master? It's probably only fair to say Floyd and me were the two best fighters of the whole army, and I already enjoyed challenging him when I was a student. I also enjoyed humiliating him. And that's where the problem lies."

"What do you mean, humiliating?"

"He occasionally lost fights against me, and people saw. Not quite the best reputation for a wannabe army leader, to lose to a student ten years his junior, right?" She took a deep breath. "We were like siblings at the start, but through the years, we almost became strangers through all the arguing. I used to nickname him Rob and he called me Neva, but... when we changed our names for each other, we also changed what we meant to each other. It was the final straw in my game of humiliating him – to use his first name – and it was his final attempt to get distance between us, that he uses my last name."

"And that is reason enough for him to want to kill you?"

She sighed insecurely. "I'm honestly not sure. There was some more stuff that happened, but the final reason was probably my betrayal."

"What's the other stuff that happened?"

Mum bit her lip, shook her head, then nodded and locked eyes with me. "He called me a whore for getting pregnant."

My heart skipped a beat in anger. "That should be more of a reason for *you* to be willing to kill *him!*"

"Oh, it is." She let out a bitter laugh. "No, what I'm referring to is that I left the army due to my pregnancy just a month or two after the war, and he had never expected me to leave that early. He'd thought I'd stay with him, help him clean up the mess the war had left in the army, but there was no way I was going to stay. I was 17! It wasn't only my child – you, it was also my own late teen years I'd lose to the army. I knew that if I stayed, I would lose everything piece by piece, so Mort and I went together. We stayed at home for the first few years of your childhood, we could live from the army salary, and then I joined the police and your dad started working as a vet."

"And Robinett? Did he ever check up on you?"

"We were on bad terms when I left, and both of us are too proud to give in to the temptation of breaking the silence. The phone call was the first time we talked in almost 17 years." She sighed. "And it doesn't seem out-of-character for his pride to want to kill me after I destroyed his perfect authority in front of the whole world. Once the war is over, once the media have nothing more to gossip about, they will absolutely *destroy* him. *How could the great army leader fail that badly? Why didn't he tell the world?*" She shook her head and hopped off the counter. "Anyway, now you know the story. If I hadn't enjoyed playing games with him, everything might be different now."

She gave me a sad smile and left the kitchen.

Thorne

Everest's innuendos were still stuck in my mind late at night, but I hadn't had another chance to talk to him alone all evening.

We'd had dinner together and spent a few hours in front of the TV, watching some quiz show that nobody really paid attention to. Just a faint distraction from all that'd been going on in the past days.

And in the morning, when I woke up early and made my way to the living room where he was supposed to be sleeping on the couch, he was gone.

I thought he had just gone to the toilet or something, but when the light of my phone flashlight wandered over the table, it met a letter with my name on it.

I turned on the ceiling lights.

Yeah, I hadn't just imagined that faint smell of a dying candle.

Right next to the envelope was one of the candles Nevada had put on a shelf in case somebody would sabotage the power of our flat.

Where had Everest gone?

My hands were shaking as I picked up the letter. It was sealed with wax. So that was what he'd needed the candle for. Typical, I thought as I broke the seal and took the letter out of the envelope.

I wasn't ready to see his handwriting again. I hadn't been ready to see *him* again. Nothing had prepared me for meeting him again.

I sank down on the sofa, wrapped myself in the blanket – which was still warm and smelled of Everest – and unfolded the paper.

My lips moved along as I silently started to read.

Dear Thorne.

Okay, this is too formal. Let's start again.

Hey babe!

Shit. I'm not allowed to call you that anymore.

Let's do this another way.

Dear finder of this letter.

Unfortunately, I have to leave this apartment due to... well, foreseen circumstances. I will not be able to help you with that grimoire.

Rosary has sent me an alchemical message demanding my presence in the Manor now, so I have to leave, but not without making a confession.

As I told you before, I have done something stupid, and I decided to tell you what it is about. You can decide yourself what you will do with that information. Tell someone or keep it to yourself.

I assume after you've read this, we won't meet anymore.

Never again.

So this is my farewell. I won't forget you, ever. If I had lipstick, I'd kiss the paper now. But I don't, so just imagine if you want to.

I just realised I haven't even explained what this is about, besides all the drama. So I'll leave you the option to never find out. But if you want to know, you may now turn the paper.

Love,

Everest

The first thing on my mind was that he seemed to never have stopped loving me. The second was the question whether Rosary knew where he'd been, and if that was the reason why he said we'd never meet again. And the third one was the urge to turn the letter to read on.

It took me maximum twenty seconds to skim over it. Half a second to drop the paper as if it was aflame. And three to pick it up again and stuff it into my pocket, for no one ever to read it again except for me.

🪷

<u>Sparrow</u>

"**M**orning, Thorne." I entered the living room.

He just stared at me from the sofa.

"You all right?" I frowned.

"He's gone," Thorne whispered. "Just gone! And he left me a letter. Rosary sent some alchemical message for him and he had to leave. He won't be able to help us today." He spoke hastily, avoiding eye contact, and I shook my head. Something was off here, but I didn't know what it was.

"So?" I just asked.

"I assume we have to go into the Manor on our own."

"Really?" Jasmine stared at us. "Why?"

I hadn't heard her come in, but Thorne didn't react surprised. He just sighed. "Everest is gone. He couldn't stay."

I still couldn't believe this story. Something was *very* off, but I couldn't tell if it was Everest's or Thorne's part of it.

"Let's wait for Nevada and Mortimer so I only have to tell the story once." He sounded genuinely insecure and tired, but so were all of us. Tired and insecure about the war.

It took only a few minutes until my parents got up as well. Something about their faces told me they'd been awake for longer already, but had cuddled and maybe cried about their fate, and it hurt so badly. Those two adults, who had thought they would never have to worry about a war again, were now back here, risking their lives.

"You're up already?" Mum smiled carefully.

We exchanged awkward looks and eventually, Thorne nodded. "I got up and found that Everest was gone."

"Gone?" Mum frowned.

"Yeah. When I came here, nobody was there, but his blanket was still warm and the candle too, as if he'd just left. And there was a letter on the table."

"Can I see it?" Mum softly asked.

Thorne flinched and shook his head – maybe a bit too fast.

"Love confessions?" My voice was sharper than intended, but I couldn't believe he was keeping that letter from us. What if there was something important in it that he hadn't understood?

"Sparrow." Mum gave me an annoyed look.

"What?" I replied, now full on adrenaline. "What if there's something important? What if Thorne missed information, the lovesick boy he is?"

"Oh shut up, you don't understand anything!" Thorne glared at me.

"Calm down, both of you," Mum said. "We have to respect Thorne's privacy. Thorne – what do you want to tell us about the letter?"

"Everest got called back to the Manor by Rosary through some alchemical message."

"Oh, I know these." Mum let out a frustrated sigh. "A cloud of alchemical dust that floats to the recipient and forms letters in the air."

"Yeah, anyway – he also said we would never meet again."

Thank God.

"Anything else?" Mum questioned.

"He won't be able to help us with the grimoire."

"That means you kids or us adults have to go there." She sighed and tilted her head. "Technically, since most Wickeds and Eternals are out on the streets and only Clarisse and Estelle are in the Manor, you could go. I'm not sure what Floyd will do to us if Mortimer and I aren't there here support the army today."

"Then we will go," I said immediately. *Everything is better than sitting around here doing nothing. Even if it's going back to the Manor.*

Mum nodded. "Alright. Have breakfast and prepare."

"Are you okay?" I frowned. "You're literally agreeing to send your child and her friends into a dangerous house with dangerous people around."

"Do I have a choice?" She gave me a tired look. "You know your way through Manor. Thorne knows the book. And your dad and I have to fight. You *know* you're not safe here alone, and possibly, you're even safer in the Manor than here. They won't expect you to be there."

"You said that about the stores too."

"If Everest hadn't been here to hypnotize the people at the door, and if you had been in here – do you think you would've stood a chance?"

"They've only attacked while you weren't here, Mrs. Morrigane," Jasmine slowly added. "What does that mean?"

Mum smiled sadly. "That, even after all these years, my reputation is still strong enough to keep them away."

BETRAYAL
Sparrow

We were ready to leave right after breakfast. There we stood, in the living room, armed and in black clothes. Nothing new.

Mum heaved her backpack onto the table and rifled through it. Her movements were slower than usual and seemed a bit off. Yeah, and she wasn't to blame. Everybody would be exhausted and tired in this situation.

Eventually, she had two vials in her hand. "I can offer you two more things. One is a potion that will make you invisible to the ban around the estate — you'll be able to cross the border at any point you want. And the other makes you invisible to people." She sighed. "Both vials hold exactly three doses, and the effects are short. You better be careful of when to use them."

I nodded and put them into one of the leg pockets of my black jeans.

"Hurry. And let us know when you're in trouble," Mum said. "Just call and we'll be there to save you."

"There's no reception on the entire estate, except for inside the Manor," Thorne replied.

"They're more likely to find you in the Manor than outside, right?" Mum said. "Now hurry."

Without another word, without any goodbyes, we left the flat, and Thorne led us through the streets. Thorne, my boyfriend, who had secrets related to his resurrected lover.

I sighed internally as I once again remembered they had never even broken up. Technically, death had parted them. Technically, it was possible that Thorne still loved him.

What if he'd always just seen me as a placeholder to fill the void inside his heart?

I had never been the girl to quickly get jealous, but with Thorne, everything had changed. He'd been my first real friend for a long time, and at the same time he was my boyfriend. I was so scared to lose both sides of him over Everest.

And Jasmine – she still saw me as younger and immature, that was for sure. But was it possible that she still had a thing for Thorne as well? At least I could be sure he wouldn't leave me for *her*. Not after what had happened at the Manor last year.

So here I was now, on a secret mission with the boy I loved that probably had mixed feelings about the reappearance of his crush, and with a girl who didn't take me seriously. In the middle of a war.

Last night, the Wickeds had killed the mayor of White Lilies Creek – a former army member. And they had started attacks all over England. It seemed like their attempt of invading this village was only the start of a terrible series of fights, but also the most dire one. There were more fighters of both the Wickeds and the army here than anywhere else, while the magical department of the police had been called to London, where there had been sightings of Wicked magic in some quarters.

When Mum had said it felt like she was in a nightmare, to me, everything had felt too real to agree with her, but now, I fully understood her. The failed rite last year had been the beginning of all this trouble – of the Eternals being back in the media and targeted by everybody, of Mum rethinking her past and looking into the war's history again, of the Eternals and the Wickeds teaming up for the fight.

It was insane.

A nightmare.

A shot, just a street further. A scream.

And before I could even think about it, my legs carried me away, as fast as I could. Thorne and Jasmine were right beside me as more and more shots were fired.

Keep us safe.

Despite growing up Christian, I hadn't prayed in years. Until now. I wasn't even sure who I prayed to. Some higher power, maybe God or Jesus or some totally different entity.

Keep us safe.

It was a mantra, nothing else on my mind than this one sentence.

Keep us safe.

And either the higher power had heard my pleading, or we were just really, really lucky. We arrived at the hip-high but magically secured wall of White Lilies Estate unharmed and without any persecutors behind us.

"It's time." I pulled out one of the vials – the one Mum had labelled as *ban-breaking potion.* "Remember – it doesn't last long. We need to get over the wall immediately after drinking it."

The others nodded and I pulled the cork off the vial. A short sip, and I climbed over the wall. The LeDouxes seemed assured nobody could ever break that ban, because there was no other obstacle than this low wall.

Thorne and Jasmine drank their portion too and followed me, and there we were. Back at White Lilies.

Thorne

We walked on in silence. I was the only one who knew the way, and I was the only one who knew what was ahead.

Sparrow let out a stifled scream when she saw the torn remainders of a tarpaulin fluttering in the wind.

"Our old lair." Jasmine's voice was hoarse. "*Your* old lair, rather. What.... What exactly did you do after I left?"

"We talked a lot," Sparrow gave back. "And we wanted to run away at Summer Solstice, however a very certain person did not make it out of the gate, so we wanted to free her first. And failed."

"It was worth it." Her voice was almost inaudible now. "You managed to be happy again together. I wouldn't ever have been happy knowing I sacrificed one of you for my own freedom."

"It took us quite a bunch of therapy sessions." I gave her a tired grin. "It's fine. You're alive again, we are here together..."

"And are gonna die if we don't hurry to get that grimoire now," Sparrow interrupted me harshly.

I flinched. "You're right. Let's walk on."

The memories had hit me harder than expected. All that had happened here, all the conversations that had been held under that torn tarpaulin, all the things I had tried to leave behind during therapy... they'd returned in an unpleasant way.

But we had different things to care about now.

I shook off the memories and hasted on, leading the girls through the forest.

And the next wave of overthinking hit me like a branch in the face.

Would we meet Everest in the Manor, or was he dead? Had Rosary found out that he'd been with us? And if not – and if we would meet him – how was I supposed to react? Talk to him as if nothing had happened, as if he hadn't just–

No way.

And I had to tell the others somehow. *Somehow.* I hated to be the bearer of bad news. I hated this news specifically. I hated what it meant, and I hated what they might cause.

What if they would hate *me*, make *me* responsible for what Everest did? How likely was that?

I remembered how Nevada had said she'd used torture. *Of course*, she'd said. Well, so had I. Before I knew it was wrong. She'd done it, fully aware of the moral falseness. And she'd indicated she would do it again. To Floyd.

So why not to me or to Everest, for what he had done and what I had kept a secret?

No way, she wouldn't make me responsible for his deeds. But if she caught *him*...

We reached the graveyard before I could consider telling them *now*. Not about my absurd fears, obviously, but about the letter.

"Hurry," Sparrow said and marched straight to the one grave under which the secret entry to the Manor was hidden. "I don't want to spend a minute more than necessary here."

We heaved the slab aside and entered the musty tunnel. It didn't scare Sparrow and me anymore, only Jasmine shivered and looked around insecurely as we hurried on.

We arrived at the torture chamber, left it before Jasmine could see too much that would upset her any further, and eventually stood in front of the library.

"What if they're inside?" Sparrow said slowly.

"Maybe it's time I'm making use of my beloved powers," Jasmine said with a sarcastic smile and before I could ask what she was talking about, she took out her hearing aids.

She winced and closed her eyes in pain, but I could only imagine what she was hearing or feeling. *Super-hearing* – was it limited to an area, or could she also hear what was going on in other parts of the manor? Could she even hear Sparrow's and my heartbeat? Either way, I could definitely understand why she was wearing the hearing aids. The noise must be driving her insane.

Jasmine smiled for a split second, as if she'd been surprised by something, then she opened her eyes again and put the hearing aids back into her ears.

"We are safe," she said. "Clarisse and Estelle are in another wing of the manor. Maybe they kitchen."

"Perfect," Sparrow said and before I could inquire what had been so surprising to Jasmine, she had already opened the door and we entered the library.

"Let's split up," I suggested. "So we can cover a larger area in less time. Remember – it's brown, black and red leather, and it says *grimoire* on the spine."

"Perfect. Good luck, everybody." Sparrow gave me a quick hug.

Oh thank God, she's not pissed because of Everest's reappearance. I let out a sign of relief, and then we split up to check the shelves.

Did they know we were looking for the grimoire? Had they hidden it already, or were they clueless? If they'd hidden it, we wouldn't stand a chance.

Lost in my thoughts, I skimmed the rows, occasionally thinking I found it, but it was just a similar one with a different title.

"Thorne!"

Three voices called my name at the same time and I spun around.

Everest, right behind me, smiling carefully.

Sparrow, at the end of the shelves, staring at me.

Jasmine, not here, yelling something.

Everest. Sparrow.

Everest, Sparrow.

The letter.

My hand slid into my pocket and a cold shock flashed through my body.

The letter was gone.

WHAT IS LOVE? (BABY DON'T HURT ME)
Thorne

Sparrow came closer with forceful steps. "Is that what you want, Thorne Phoenix Kyril LeDoux? Is that what you want? *Him?* Supporting a traitor? Kiss him, finally, and tell me it's over!" She raised her hands and smashed mine and Everest's foreheads against each other.

Dizziness numbed my mind. "Sparrow~"

"Fuck you. Both of you. Just go fuck yourself. Or each other. I couldn't care less." Her voice trembled as she threw the letter on the ground in front of me. "It's over. Everything is over. Your boyfriend has poisoned my mother and you aren't even considering telling her! If I hadn't found the letter~"

"Stolen!" Her implications and accusations filled me with fury. "You have *stolen* the letter! Not *found!*" My voice broke with a sob.

"Stolen, fine." She gave me a derogatory look. "And you're a traitor. We're both criminals, but maybe that's the only thing we've got in common, after all."

"Sparrow~"

"Shut up. Just save your breath." She turned on her heels and walked away.

Who knows where to.

"You're an absolutely idiot," Jasmine commented and came over to pick up the letter. She must've heard the argument and so I couldn't care less for whether she'd read it or not.

Whether she'd find out what Everest's story really was like.

That he had found the books – the one about the resurrected teens' tasks and my diary – but hadn't had time to read them before his next assignment, so he'd just stuffed them in his bag and set off to the task.

That this very certain task had been to poison Nevada Morrigane.

That only after fulfilling that task, he'd read the books, regained his memory and understood how wrong he had been.

That this had been the original reason for coming to our flat, but he hadn't had the power to tell Nevada in person, and so he'd left me the letter and disappeared.

It didn't matter anymore.

"You two'll be alright," Everest said and pulled me into his arms, but I just stood as stiff as a statue. Sparrow screaming at me had left me with the impression we'd never be alright again. She was right about many things, but not all.

I *had* planned to tell Nevada.

I had *not* planned to get back with Everest.

And now, I had lost her.

In the past, I had always thought that her death would be the worst thing that could happen between us, but now I understood this was almost worse. She was alive, but she hated me.

For a good reason.

Jasmine gave me the letter back and I pushed Everest away a bit more forcefully than intended.

"You know," Jasmine said, "if you're quick, you might be able to explain things to Sparrow before she murders you."

"I like your irony, but it's useless right now," Everest gave back. "Thorne is in a difficult situation because of me. Stupid comments don't seem too helpful."

"You remind me of her," Jasmine replied, slowly shaking her head.

She was right. Sparrow and Everest would have made great friends in any other situation.

"They're coming!" Sparrow was back with us all of a sudden. "Estelle and Clarisse are coming this way!"

"The back exit?" I didn't wait for a reply to sprint to the other end of the library.

"Where *is* the exit?" Jasmine hissed.

"They've~ fuck!" My gaze strayed around hastily. "They've blocked it with shelves!"

"Here." Sparrow gave Jasmine the vial with the invisibility potion. "Drink. Quick!"

Her gaze wandered from me to Everest and back, as if she was calculating- yes! There were four of us now, and the potion was only for three...

"Take mine." I held the vial towards her as Jasmine gave it to me.

"Definitely not." She didn't even look into my eyes as she let out a bitter laugh. "Give it to your lover."

"Sparrow-" Everest stared at her. "They don't know I'm on your side."

"You're lying." She sounded indifferent. "They know. You've been hiding here from them, haven't you? They're gonna kill you when they find you."

"How do you know-"

"Don't talk, drink! You're all such idiots here." She let out a deep sigh, took a step back and faded into the shadows.

"Everest-" I gave him the vial with shaking hands. There was no way to convince Sparrow, and she was safe as long as she stayed in the shadows of the shelves.

Lastly, I downed the rest of the potion and put the vial into my pocket. "We need to try and get out through the main exit," I mumbled. It felt weird to talk to invisible people – as if nobody was here. "We need to stay in the shadows, for Sparrow. Let's see how far to the exit we can get, and then... maybe we just have to run. We'll meet in the flat."

"Great plan" Sparrow said bitterly. "Just like all of your plans."

"Let's go," I just said and snuck to the front row of the shelves. The door was only a few meters away, but it was closed and the two women were standing at a window, assumingly seeing the door from the corner of their eyes.

They slowly turned away, talking lowly, and walked further into the library, and that was the moment.

"Run!" I hissed and when the two women turned around, I hasted to the door, slammed it open against the wall and ran down the hallway. No clue if anyone was following me – friend or foe.

Out of the main door, over the cobblestones, out through the brass gate, and towards freedom.

It had almost been too easy, I thought, but then I remembered we didn't have the grimoire. And Sparrow still hated me.

"Guys?" I carefully asked into the blue. "Anyone with me?"

"I'm here." Sparrow appeared out of the shadows of a house. "Though I don't know where you are. And I'm not sure if I want to know."

"Sparrow..."

"Yeah, I know, you wanna talk, blah, blah." She shook her head. "But what if I don't?"

"Then I will beg you to listen." I struggled to keep my emotions in check. I'd rather scream at her, try to make her understand my point, but it would be even more in vain than anything else I would try to do.

"Then tell me," she said provokingly. "Tell me why you didn't say anything about the poison. You were afraid I would hate Everest for it, weren't you? You were afraid I would blame you for his deeds. Isn't that the truth?"

"I think *you* are afraid I would leave you for Everest," I gave back in a calm voice.

"And you think this mistrust got any better with you hiding what he did?" She let out a bitter laugh. "How idiotic."

"I wanted to tell you, I swear," I said as normally as possible. "Both you and your mother. But do you have any idea how hard it is to tell somebody they've been *poisoned?*"

"You could have just given her the letter."

"And she would have read it, become shocked and lost focus in the fights. And you'd have made me responsible for her death."

Sparrow kept silent for a moment. "What proves you were really planning to tell her?"

"I can't prove it. You just have to believe me."

"I'm not sure you understand my point. It's not the fact that Everest poisoned Mum that hurts me most.

That's between him and Mum, not between you and me. It's the fact that you kept it to yourself that's way worse. I see where you're coming from, trying to protect her *mentally*, but she is literally born for this type of bad news. She's a *fighter!*"

"You know just as well as I do that this is plain wrong. She is *weak*, she's not the young girl she once was in her army times."

"Yeah, she's got to care for us now and it's breaking her," Sparrow gave back, but in her restless eyes, I could read that that was just as worried about Nevada as I was.

"So?" I just said.

"I don't know. I don't know anything anymore. You've messed me up." She closed her eyes and pressed her fingers against her temples as if she had migraine. Opening her eyes again, she spoke on. "You know I love you. But this~ this has broken the trust between us. Maybe my jealousy has done the same. Maybe we are both guilty. But how can we continue this?" She hesitated. "Do we even *want* to continue this relationship?"

Her words hit me like a damned truck on these Victorian streets. "Is that... a rhetorical question?"

"Absolutely not." She sighed. "Listen, Thorne, you need to make your decision. Everest or me. I won't be offended if you pick him. Not offended. Just hurt, but that is fine. Hurt me once by leaving, but don't pretend to love me and hurt me again with every lie."

"I-"

"Or if you love me more than him, why did you have to break my trust?"

"I just-"

"Can't you for once let me finish my dramatic monologue?"

"Fine- sorry."

"Now I forgot what I wanted to say. Great." She massaged her temples.

"I only love *you* this way," I said under my breath before she could say anything else. "Romantically, I mean. Everest is still a friend who I love dearly, but not romantically. It's been over between us since his death."

Silence.

"I swear to God, if you are lying to me again..." Her voice broke, and maybe it was better that way. I didn't even want to hear about her eternal wrath.

"You're turning visible again," she then said almost mindlessly, took a step forward and kissed me.

Needless to say, I almost fainted at her touch. All the fear of losing her fell off of me in that one second and made me dizzy, maybe a bit lovesick.

Until the moment was over and we returned to the flat without another word.

WHAT FLOWERS MEAN
Sparrow

Why?
Because I loved him. Even after all he had done.

Because he still meant the world to me.

And because we had to resolve this issue before any of us were going to die in the war.

I wondered where Jasmine and Everest were. Had they made it to the flat?

Ever since I'd heard Clarisse and Estelle talking about him in the hallway on their way to the library, I felt worried about him. A feeling I'd never thought I'd have, for him of all people. But he *had* been unaware. He *had* trusted the LeDouxes. We all had, at some point, even for a whole year. Not once in the time they'd been our host family, we had assumed they were *killers*. Yeah, they had been weird, but they had electricity and mobile phones just like every normal modern family, and I had always assumed they were some kind of extreme role-players. Looking back on it, though... I had never actually seen any of them *use* a phone or electricity of any kind. It had all been a part of the show they'd prepared for the teens.

For us.

We arrived at the hotel. Every step on the steep stairs was more reluctant, more fearful. I didn't want to arrive to Dad, in tears, sitting on the sofa with men in black suits and white gloves.

But there'd have been a black limousine, in that case, right?

Or maybe they'd both died in the war.

Impossible. This couldn't have happened.

Don't get a panic attack now.

My hands trembled and white stars flickered in front of my eyes as we arrived in front of the flat door, where Jasmine and Everest were sitting on the ground.

Right – I had the key.

So neither Mum nor Dad was there. Was this a good sign?

I bit my lip to stay in the moment, to not let fear and memories take over, until I tasted the metallic blood.

"Thank God, you're there." Jasmine got up.

"Of course. You won't get rid of us that easily." My voice sounded so far away and I struggled to get the key into the lock.

And eventually, I sank down onto the sofa. The white sparkles slowly faded as I poured myself a glass of coke and drank it at once.

"Everything was in vain," Thorne slowly said and joined me. "Everything."

"Not exactly." Jasmine hesitated. "I found something between the shelves." She held up a little note. "I'm not sure what it is or means, but..."

Within a second, we were all behind her, looking at the note.

To Estelle ~ Grimoire recipe. Three mixed zinnia blossoms. Three cyclamen blossoms. Three leaves of narrow leaf cattail. One rhizanthella blossom. A bunch of monkshood.

"What the heck is this supposed to mean?" Thorne frowned.

"Some alchemical mess, maybe?" Jasmine turned to me. "Your mother knows a lot about potions, right?"

"It's her magic power," I mumbled. *Mum.* The thought hit me hard again. I had to tell her about the poison as soon as possible, but could I just call her? What if she was right in the middle of a fight? How fast would the poison work? Was it deadly or just supposed to make her ill? How did Everest even manage to give it to her without her realising?

"Do you think she can work with this?" Jasmine asked on.

"I'm not sure. I assume so..."

"What if it *isn't* alchemical?" Everest suggested. "Maybe it's just a placeholder for a secret message. We should consider all options."

"That's true." Jasmine raised the paper to the ceiling lights, to check if there was anything hidden. "Nothing."

"Let's hold it over a candle." Everest went to the shelf and grabbed one of the emergency candles.

☙ 🕷 ❧

We spent the next hour looking up different forms of coding and decoding messages and applying them to the paper, but in vain.

"Then it has to be alchemical," Jasmine said. "We need to ask Nemo as soon as she is back."

"I hear my name?"

"Mum!" I turned around to face the door. "You're early."

"Yeah, Floyd sent me home after I got lightly injured." She shook her head. "He really wants to get that revenge himself, trying to keep me safe in that war."

Yeah, after all you told me about him, that sounds right.

"He's insane," Thorne mumbled. "How can one person be as cruel as he is?"

"I mean, it's fair," Mum said. "He will be put on trial as well, once the war is over. But not an army trial. A real one, by the government, for hiding everything. And I know him well enough to see that he wants to take revenge before spending the rest of his life in prison."

"That doesn't justify anything!" Thorne gave back.

Well, yeah, maybe it does from his perspective.

Mum and I exchanged a look. "Forget it for the moment." She made a gesture as if to wave away the thought. "There are more important things now."

Yeah, your death.

"Are you aware that in the past few hours, all the remaining schools have been attacked?" Mum said. "It is safe to assume that something is going to happen soon. Maybe they're calling their fighters here. Did you..." She stopped herself when she saw our disappointed faces.

"We didn't find the grimoire," Jasmine confessed. "But we found a note." She gave Mum the note, and Mum frowned and pushed her glassed down to the tip of her nose.

For a pretty long time, she said nothing.

Maybe she was calculating what to do with these amounts and plants, or maybe she was recalling images of them.

"That's literally *nothing*," she eventually said. "Nothing that could make a potion to help us, I mean. It's just a mix of random flowers that don't mean anything!"

"Flowers?" Thorne flinched. "What if they *do* mean something?"

Victorian flower language was a common way to encode messages from one person to another. Unlike common belief, it dealt not only with love confessions, but with all topics of life, and thus it was no surprise that Thorne had found a translation for the first plant online within seconds.

"Mixed zinnia stands for thinking of an absent friend. Which, in our case, could be the grimoire. It isn't in the library, so it is absent."

"Sounds right." Mum stretched and got up from her armchair. "Let me know when you've translated the whole text. I'm gonna prepare dinner, Mort will arrive any second."

This was my chance. I jumped up and followed her to the kitchen. "Let me help you!"

Mum frowned and closed the kitchen door. "Alright, what do you want to talk about?"

"How~"

"You would never quit solving a riddle with your friends to prepare dinner instead." She gave me an exhausted smile. "So, what's all this about?"

Her sudden directness overwhelmed me and I hesitated.

"Alright, take your time." She handed me a bunch of tomatoes. "If you're here, you can actually help me, can't you? We're gonna make pasta with tomato sauce."

"Alright." I reached for a knife and started to chop the tomatoes, but stopped abruptly when she sat down at the kitchen table to mix other ingredients. The realisation hit me like stones.

"You're weak!" I blurted out.

Mum flinched, but didn't say anything.

"Do you know why?" My voice trembled. "Do you even have a clue you're not just exhausted?"

"How'd you know?" she said under her breath. "Of course I know, but I didn't know *you* knew."

"You *know* about the poison?" My voice broke.

"Somebody poured it into my drink. It was the day I met Floyd outside the city. He'd brought wine. Probably to celebrate the torture he'd put me through. We got attacked and I put my glass away to have both hands free to fight off the attackers, and when I returned and took a sip, I tasted it. Hemlock mixed with some other plants to delay the effect for some time."

"If you know it *that* specifically, why don't you do anything against it?" I stared at her.

She lowered her head. "What can I do if there's no antidote known?"

OF BASEBALL BATS AND PAIN
Sparrow

Alright, so there was no antidote known. Something had delayed the effects of hemlock. And Mum took it with an incredible mental strength.

I took a deep breath and put down the knife I'd been holding. "How long do you have left?"

"I don't know, Birdie." Mum stretched her hand out towards me and caressed my cheek. "A few hours? Days? Who knows...? The paralysing effects have become worse today with every passing hour."

"You didn't return home because of an injury, right?"

"I returned because I am too weak to fight."

"And Robinett–"

"Floyd knows about it. He was the first person I told about it, right after I'd drunk the poison and understood what had happened." She gave me a sad smile. "We had a deep conversation, just like when we were younger, like brother and sister. Just with the threat of him wanting to kill me, but we somehow put that aside for the moment. I think he was seriously struggling to think of an antidote, just so he could kill me himself, after the war." She let out a bitter laugh. "Anyway, today, I told him I was too weak, and he let me go. Without any torture or deals. He just let me go.

I just had to make something up for you, and his hate for me seemed the perfect excuse."

"When did you plan to tell us?" A hot tear ran down my cheek.

"I don't know. I–" Her voice broke. "I'm glad you found out. How...?"

"Everest." I could hardly say his name. "He was the one who did it."

A confused expression flashed over Mum's face, just for a second, then she was smiling again. "At least he found the right path again afterwards."

"You're not angry?"

"Of course not. It wasn't his fault." She took a deep breath. "Listen, Birdie, whatever will happen... You have to keep on fighting. Find the grimoire and kill the Eternals. End the war. And tell Floyd that I paid for both our guilt. But please, never stop fighting. Stay strong. For me."

"For you," I whispered and sank into her arms.

It was only then that I realised she wasn't afraid of dying. She was only afraid of leaving us behind. Of leaving Dad and me alone, alone in that big old house with our four cats and Rain. Or maybe of leaving all of us alone in this fight.

The only thing Nevada Morrigane was afraid of was having to leave her loved ones behind.

The main door of our flat collided with the wall. Mum and I flinched and sat up straight again. A voice hollered something incomprehensive, followed by screams and a crash.

"That's Mortimer." Mum gave me a grave look. "He doesn't know yet. Don't talk to him. I swear I will tell him, but–"

"Tell him *what*?"

Dad.

"Tell him that we are getting attacked while you're here– crying?" He frowned. "What is going on here?"

Shots in the living room. I barely noticed them. The kitchen was like a safe bubble, our own space, where nothing could harm us. Just Mum, Dad, me, and the unspoken secret between us.

"Nothing." Mum got up. "Absolutely nothing."

"You're lying to me, Nevada!"

More shots and screams. The bubble exploded and panic washed over me, took hold of me.

"Run, Sparrow!" Mum screamed at me. "Run! Save yourself!"

"But–"

"I won't be much of a help anyway anymore!" She pushed me towards the door. "And maybe they will make it quicker than the poison."

The blood rushed in my ears and I no longer heard anything. The walls moved and twisted as I stumbled into the living room, right into some guy with a gun. He was dead on the ground a second later, my gun was in my hand. For a moment, I saw Cecily and Clarisse, hand in hand, swinging baseball bats towards me. And from that point on, I remembered nothing.

ॐ 🕷 ॐ

Looking back on it, I couldn't tell anymore what had been a hallucination and what had been real. Cecily and Clarisse, hand in hand, swinging baseball bats? Sounded unreal. However – could I have really hallucinated the details, the thick bandage around Cecily's hand?

And the dead guy – he must have had a face, but my mind refused to recall the memory, called him the Faceless instead. A trauma reaction. Which indicated I'd really killed him. Maybe I'd also killed several people, which would explain the hallucinations. Or somebody had sprayed toxic gas, drugs – or I'd had a panic attack.

The only thing that was vivid and real was the conversation with Mum.

And that was exactly what I told Thorne, Jasmine and Everest when we met again somewhere in White Lilies Creek.

I had no memories of how I'd gotten to this random street crossing, but I had probably just followed the others.

"And your parents?" Everest asked after I'd summarized what had happened. "Do you remember them?"

Of course I remembered my parents! I hadn't forgotten my whole life, only the escape! Oh – that was probably what he meant. I shook my head to get rid of the numb, distanced feeling.

"You don't know what happened to them?" he inquired.

"Oh, I do know. They're in the hands of the Wickeds and Eternals." My voice sounded so far away. "What- what exactly happened?"

"Your dad came in, through the door," Jasmine said and knelt down in front of me. I hadn't even realised I was sitting on the concrete. "He was followed by a bunch of Wickeds and Eternals, and he didn't stand a chance to block them from coming in. We fought them off for a while, when he went to alarm you and your mother... and then you came into the living room, alone, straight up shot a guy and leaped out of the window to float downstairs. And that's when we decided to follow you. I will never again climb down a facade from the third floor, no matter how ornate and easy to climb it is."

So it had been me who had declared fleeing would be the best way. The famous fight-or-flight instinct.

It had been for the best, probably. We wouldn't have stood a chance. At least we weren't dead yet.

Had they killed Mum and Dad already, right there in the flat? Had they taken away Mum's pain? It didn't seem like something they'd do.

No matter how hard I tried to focus on those questions, the image in my mind didn't fade.

The image of the dead guy on the ground.

And Jasmine had confirmed it'd been me who killed him.

"We know where the grimoire is," Thorne eventually said, distracting me from the horrifying imagery. "But we should get help. It might be a trap."

"Where is it?" My voice trembled.

"Down in the catacombs by the lagoon. Some plants hinted at danger and the absence of the grimoire again, and the last two are common lagoon plants. That can't be a coincidence."

"Could be a trap, too," I said hollowly. "We're not going there alone."

The others stared at me as if I'd lost my mind.

"You don't wanna-" Thorne shook his head. "He's gonna kill you!"

"Better him than the LeDouxes, right?" I bit my lip and the metallic taste of blood filled my mouth again.

"Thorne, there's no other way. We have to ask Floyd Robinett and the army for help."

❧ 🕷 ☙

We hasted through the streets, back to the place we'd come from.

When Mum and Floyd had phoned, he'd been in that building opposite of our flat, so maybe he still was there. Or anyone of the army.

Though – somehow I hoped he'd be there himself. There had to be a reason why he'd been the army leader for twenty years – personal hatred was the one thing, but other than that, I assumed him to be a competent man.

At least at times when he didn't want to kill me.

No, he *had* to help us. A victory was as much his goal as it was ours.

And still – we'd tricked him again. He knew nothing about the grimoire, and I had no clue how he would react upon hearing of it.

We reached the flat at dusk. From the outside, it seemed to have been a ruin for years, but the door was locked. And there was no bell.

Jasmine pulled out a hairpin, the door swung open and she smiled. "What are you waiting for?"

I went first, up the stairs.

Housebreaking. Another crime against the army.

The flat on the third floor was locked as well and Jasmine opened it.

Maybe this was the best strategy – to surprise and confuse him. Or maybe, he'd shoot us immediately. Then, everything was lost anyway.

Wasn't everything lost anyway?

Mum and Dad were possibly dead already, and we stood little to no chance. Was there even a reason for fighting left?

The door swung open.

Nothing happened.

The flat was empty, totally empty. No furniture, no traces of army members. Apparently, Floyd Robinett hadn't spent much time here, maybe he had just stalked Mum from here.

"What now?" Jasmine asked. "Is there anything left but to go to the lagoon? We can only hope to find the book before they find us."

We exchanged looks.

"Okay," I finally said. "Let's find that fucking boob and finish them."

&ρ 🕷 ᔆ

Jasmine

We hasted down the stairs, out of the building, and through the nocturnal streets. I didn't know why we were running – maybe it was the general panic or the knowledge we were on our own now.

While we were running, pictures flashed through my mind. Pictures of the city, of a cinema, of my parents. Pictures I wasn't supposed to see.

Pictures of my past.

I had to stop and take a few deep breaths. This was impossible. How did I know this, all of a sudden? Okay, Everest had remembered things too, but he had had much more information. He'd had Thorne's entire diary.

"Jasmine?" Thorne returned to me. "What are you waiting for?"

"I... I remember." My glance strayed away, to the night sky, and – "The fog has almost vanished. The city is almost entirely Victorian. And I remember more and more pieces of my past."

"You think these things are related?" Everest joined us.

"I think it's all related..." I hesitated. "The fog is above the quarters that haven't been turned Victorian yet. The fog first faded when I began to remember, and it's become way less foggy since you started to remember as well." I nodded towards Everest. "The more memories are restored, the less fog there is and the more Victorian quarters, and the less fog there is, the more memories are restored. So as soon as one of us starts to remember – in this case you and me – it's a chain reaction."

"So you mean all of the resurrected teens will remember their past?" Sparrow stared at me. "Maybe it will even happen tonight, then! I bet the LeDouxes are planning–"

"It *is* a trap," Thorne said slowly. "The letter about the grimoire. It is a trap. They want us there so they can finish their revenge. But we can't avoid going down to the lagoon if we want to stand *any* chance of getting the book."

"Who says the book is even there, then?" I gave back.

"Because if we see they don't have it, we can just turn around and run." Sparrow crossed her arms. "I suggest we hurry. The sooner this is over, the better."

Everest nodded. "And just in case they have some of the resurrected teens there... don't look into anyone's eyes or they can hypnotize you. Just the tiniest bit of eye contact, and if you aren't focused on resisting, you're a lost cause."

"Do you think they..." Sparrow hesitated. "They might have hypnotized my parents, too? Instead of killing them?"

"Honestly, I doubt it." I let out a bitter laugh. "They want them to suffer."

"I don't know if that is good or bad." Sparrow sighed. "Alright, so we have to hurry, don't look anybody in the eyes, and we can technically kill the Wickeds, but not the Eternals as long as we don't have the grimoire. Anything I missed?"

"Don't think so." Thorne took her hand. "Let's run."

WHITE LILIES DEATH
Thorne

I led the others to the coast, and when we arrived, I took a moment to just stand there and look across the vast beauty of the moonlit sea.

"Let's climb down the basalt pillars," Everest suggested.

"We will arrive right in the cave where Cecily tried to murder Nevada," I added. Next to me, Sparrow flinched.

I put my arm around her shoulder. "And with a little luck, the book will be right there; we can grab it and run up here again."

Of course, that was a desperate, silly bit of hope. How unrealistic.

"It's time," Everest said. He looked at me and jumped down pillar by pillar as if it was just a normal stairway.

"He's right." Sparrow shrugged and followed him just as elegantly, and Jasmine nudged me. "You clearly have a type."

I blushed, but didn't protest. It was nothing but the truth.

We followed Sparrow and Everest down to the sea level, walked along the beach until the basalt was replaced with chalkstones, and there we stood in front of the exit through which Cecily had stumbled in pain and fallen right into the sea.

"I'll go first." Sparrow raised her gun and her phone flashlight and made her way inside. I was right behind her, my own gun ready to shoot at anyone who would try to hurt us.

The flashlights of three phones – Everest didn't own one – wandered over the rough chalk walls, but I didn't really take care where my light went. I saw everything anyway. From down here, the hall was even huger, and it took me some time to find the hole in the ceiling through which we'd observed Cecily's murder attempt.

I imagined how maybe, here had been a lair of the army in the wars. There was the exit outside and the tunnels into all directions to keep open all possibilities to escape. Maybe they'd had tents to sleep in, and had made fires below the hole in the ceiling so the smoke could move off. And maybe, they'd fought here. Maybe, people had died here.

Maybe, people would die here today again.

Maybe we would die.

"There's something in the hallway," Jasmine whispered and pointed to the one to the left, which was completely in the darkness.

I'd almost laughed aloud. What had to look like a strange thing in a tunnel to her wasn't even a tunnel. It was just an indentation in the wall, no broader or deeper than a small wooden lectern. Which might seem like a weird measuring unit, but it was the most obvious one because, well, that *was* exactly what was in that indentation. A small wooden lectern with a book in a red, brown, black cover that said *grimoire*.

Sparrow reached out for the book and carefully lifted it.

"We made it!" she whispered.

"Most definitely."

We spun around. And there they were.

<u>Sparrow</u>

They filled the room, one by one.

Strangers.

Eternals, who wanted to see us dead for ruining the rite last year.

Wickeds, who wanted revenge for the injustice of the war and for the army keeping their knowledge of said injustice a secret.

Then familiar faces.

Rosary. Estelle. Thill. Kyle with Ethan. Clarisse and Cecily, hand in hand. Without baseball bats, but Cecily with a thick bandage around her right hand.

The two archenemies, united against a common enemy.

Us.

And they weren't alone.

About 50 teens and twice as many adults stood behind them. Four of them were holding Mum and Dad.

At least they were still alive.

"Cecilia Williams, stop this chaos immediately!"

All heads turned to the exit we had entered through.

"Robinett?" Cecily laughed. She laughed, and she didn't stop for a solid minute. Then, she said, "It's incredible you still give me commands, and it's even more incredible that you still believe I'll obey. After all you did to me and my families. After all the secrets you kept from the world. You *knew* we were innocent, and you never apologized! Neither to us nor to the rest of the world. Not even to your own people!" She pointed to Mum ~ Mum, who didn't even have power to raise her head anymore.

"Were you afraid?", Cecily continued provokingly. "Were you afraid to lose your position? To be made fun of for your stupidity? You're *weak*, Robinett, and now you're all alone. Because even your *sister* chose to betray you."

Thorne whispered something to me, but I shook my head. This wasn't the situation to discuss Mum and Floyd.

"Everybody makes mistakes, Cecilia, and it certainly was a mistake to keep it all a secret." Floyd Robinett gave her a pleading look. "You still have the chance to stop this, and we can find a peaceful solution. Nobody has to die tonight. Let go of your ties to the Eternals – Wasn't it them who started the war?"

Him, trying to find a peaceful solution?

This didn't sound like the Floyd I'd gotten to know. Did he change for Cecily?

Something was wrong here, very wrong, and I wasn't talking about all the weapons that were pointed at us.

"You said it yourself, Sir," Clarisse said. "Everybody makes mistakes. And ours was to not work with Cecily and her people from day one on. In the last days, she's been more loyal to us than she's ever been to you."

"You want a peaceful solution, after all this?" Cecily shook her head. "Are all army members that weak and naive?" She looked at Mum, then turned back to Robinett. "I mean, I assume so. It was so easy to hypnotize you – even if the effects are apparently fading sooner than we hoped – and it was so easy to make you and your people believe we were sending an alchemical bomb to the centre of London. And here you are, all alone and back in your own mind, thinking you can stop us with a bit of positive talking."

Hypnotized?

"I should have known." Mum's weak voice echoed through the hall and my heart skipped a beat. I hadn't even dared to hope I'd hear her voice again.

"You should." Robinett gave her a faint smile. "I know our last weeks together weren't great, and then 17 years of silence – but I never meant it that way. Neva, I don't want to kill you. I don't want you to die. I'm so sorry for attacking you and your daughter – they controlled me. Please, forgive me. Aren't you my sister, after all?"

So was this the real Floyd? At least Mum seemed convinced, and she was the one to know.

She nodded slowly. "You made mistakes, Floyd," she whispered. "But you're still my brother."

Robinett gave her a thankful smile. "I may be alone," he said then to the assembly of foes, "but I stand here in the name of the entire army and–"

"Not for much longer." Cecily reached out into the crowd behind her and someone handed her a machine gun.

Robinett paled.

"Floyd!" Mum screamed hoarsely. "Run!"

But it was too late.

Floyd Robinett was dead before the echo of Mum's voice had faded.

The shots had been deafening, but so was the following silence.

Cecily had blindly fired the shots and there was no chance he'd survived that.

I looked to Mum.

She'd buried her face in her hands, maybe she was crying. *Of course*, she was crying. Of course, she mourned the loss of her brother.

I hesitated, then I looked to Robinett's corpse on the ground. Whatever I had expected – a totally distorted body – it wasn't that bad. Or the last year had made me numb.

Cecily had spared his face, thankfully. This might have saved me from the worst nightmares.

If I'd survive, that was.

"Next," Cecily said and smiled, and all heads turned to us. Was she crazy? Killed a man and smiled. Could she really ignore a murder that easily, be happy about her revenge?

Maybe, it was normal in the army. Mum had said murder was normal in the army. When she'd talked about killing Floyd. When she'd been convinced he'd want to kill her. What had been a lie.

Dizziness took hold of me again.

If he hadn't been hypnotized- maybe Mum and him had worked together again. Maybe he would have come here together with us, maybe he'd long killed Cecily. Maybe he wouldn't have died.

Not another panic attack.

Time to act.

I cleared my throat. "I have the book."

"We can see that," Rosary gave back. The carving knife was there, in her belt, but right now, she was pointing an old revolver at me.

I took a deep breath. "And I will not hesitate to destroy it." I raised my own gun and pressed the barrel to the cover.

"Then you will lose every chance to win the war."

"And you will lose every chance to perform any more rites."

"And you will lose every chance to save your mother."

"What?" I stared at Rosary, then at my mother, who frantically shook her head.

"There is an antidote to hemlock poisoning in the grimoire." Rosary smiled and took the knife into her other hand. "An antidote you won't find anywhere else. You don't even know what other poisons besides hemlock were in our cocktail. But if you open that book now, you'll be dead before you can even find the correct page."

Okay, yeah, with all the snipers there, that wasn't too unrealistic, but I didn't feel fear anymore. Either we would die or win.

"And if you don't lower your weapons now, I will destroy the book."

"And if you try to run away with the book, we will kill your parents." Rosary flipped the carving knife in her hand.

"And if you kill my parents, I will kill you. Or, you know what? I'll do that regardless of what you do. We can continue to play this game, or we can do something now." I closed my eyes for a second. It was all in my hands, the exit to the sea was unblocked. Just a few steps, and I could make it.

Maybe I'd survive, or they'd shoot me right away.

The only thing that kept Rosary from killing us was the hope to torture us a bit beforehand, and I preferred the quick way of dying.

"Run," Mum yelled and locked eyes. "Sparrow, I don't have a chance anyway!"

She was right. If I ran with the book, she would be murdered. If I gave the book away, she would die from the poison and all of us would be murdered.

If I ran now, I could at least save the rest of the world. And still, it was impossible. *Heaven, help.*

"I'm sorry, Mum," I whispered, and then I ran.

A scream ringing in my ears, then silence.

The cold air of the night stinging my face, then numbness.

What had I done?

MERCY?
Sparrow

Athousand thoughts flashed through my mind, but I blocked them all out. I had the book, I just needed to hide somewhere to cast the spells. As fast as possible.

As I rushed up the basalt pillars, screams and footsteps followed me. Who was it? Friend or enemy, I didn't know. I had the book in one hand, and the gun in the other, and I was ready to use both of them. Two deadly weapons.

Mum.

What had I done?

My feet carried me over the cobblestone alleyways, towards the estate and I didn't even know why. Maybe because that was the place where they would least expect me. But it didn't matter, they were following me anyway.

What had I done?

I fused with the shadows as I hasted onto the White Lilies estate, in between the trees, and towards the graveyard. I still heard their steps cracking sticks and crunching shed leaves somewhere behind me. The full moon brightened my way, forcing me to become visible every now and then.

And then I decided to stop. I could run on forever or just hide now and hope they'd pass me by. I leaped over the graveyard wall, rolled off on the grit and lay silent for a few minutes, tightly clenching the book.

No steps passed me by, but they didn't come closer either.

Finally, I opened the book to flip through the pages, skimming the headlines until I found the page that said, *Spell to reverse immortality and kill anyone who is under the influence of life-extending potions within the next five minutes.*

A silhouette blocked the moon and threw shadows on the pages. I raised my head as steps crunched on the grit. And there she stood, right in front of me, the carving knife reflecting the wild flickering in her eyes. Rosary LeDoux.

Behind her all the others. Teens and adults. Wickeds and Eternals. Thorne, Jasmine, Everest – held captive by the other LeDouxes. Dad – and Mum! Mum! My heart skipped a beat. She was alive! Blood covered her face and clung to her hair, but she was alive!

"Prepare to die," Rosary said, raised the knife and knelt down beside me.

I could feel my hasty heartbeat unnaturally clear as I raised the book and read out the phrases, the same second as the knife darted into my shoulder.

The pain shot through my body, again and again, until Rosary seemed to understand what I had done.

My sharpened senses perceived in slow motion how the bloody knife hit the ground. Subtle blood drips sprayed on the grit as Rosary arose from the stones, her eyes widened in shock for a moment.

Then, her formerly bewildered grimace turned to a lunatic smile as she took a sheet of paper from her pocket and unfolded it. It looked as if she had just torn it out of a book. The book.

My gaze flashed between the grimoire and Rosary, who proceeded to speak. "And if it is the last thing I will do, I will make sure that my revenge is ensured."

She held up the paper and turned to the audience, then to me, so that we could read the headline. Then, still smiling, she took out a match and in all peace of mind, set the paper on fire.

The headline was visible for another second, then the paper dissolved and the wind carried off the ashes.

And still, the words were engraved in my mind.

Antidote to hemlock poisoning.

Still smiling, Rosary's body disintegrated, leaving behind nothing but the blossom of a white lily on the grit graveyard ground.

What had I done?

Thorne

As Thill's tight grip disappeared, I stumbled forward in shock, over to Sparrow. Nobody even attempted to stop me.

Together with the LeDouxes, a whole lot of Eternals had disappeared, had left white lily blossoms on the graveyard ground – and as expected, I, too, had felt the stabbing pain in my stomach. But I had survived.

I reached Sparrow at the same time as Nemo.

"Thorne." She struggled to sit up. On the right side, her shirt was drenched with blood and dark red sprinkled covered her face like freckles.

"You saved us!" I didn't dare to hug her. Didn't even want to hear what she had to say, what Rosary's knife had done to her.

"Thorne, Mum…" Her voice trembled. "I don't wanna die. Not now. Not after we won."

"You're not gonna die, okay? Sparrow–" I grabbed her hands. "You're not gonna die!"

"I'm so sorry," she whispered. "Mum, I'm so sorry." She blinked a tear away, then she sank into my arms.

"No! Sparrow!" I stared at her in despair. She couldn't have–

"Thorne–" Nevada nudged me softly, a vial in her hands, and pointed to the night sky.

The last wisps of fog faded and revealed a serene night.

Behind us, whispers got louder.

The teens remembered.

꙳ 🕷 ꙳

Sparrow

I blinked.

Where was I? I was lying somewhere. Above me was the full moon and below me a hard ground.

"Thank God, she's awake!"

Thorne.

"Are you okay, Birdie?"

Mum.

I tried to sit up. My right shoulder gave in under the pressure and I fell back to the ground. Four hands grabbed my arms immediately and supported me so I could lean against the wall of the cemetery.

A weird taste spread in my mouth, like herbs or… "Mum, did you…" I coughed and the grassy taste mixed with blood. With every breath, my ribs burned like fire.

"Yes," Mum said and wiped a strand of hair from my face. "I gave you one of my strengthening potions I still had in my pocket. Are you feeling better?"

"I think so."

"Does your shoulder still hurt?" Thorne asked.

"I got stabbed, idiot. Obviously it still hurts."

"Good to know you're still sassy as always." Thorne grinned.

"Where... where are the others?" Only now I realised we were alone on the estate.

"All the Eternals just disappeared." Mum pointed to the lilies that were spread across the cemetery. "And the teens remembered. Dad, Everest and Jasmine informed them and they helped to bring the Wickeds down into the city, into the opera. The army should be here soon too, but I doubt we still need them. Barely anyone resisted. I assume..." Her eyes glazed over for a second. "I assume we won. In a war without winners."

Wow, we had really won. I had won. I had killed the LeDouxes, and yet I felt neither pride nor relief.

"Mum..." I looked up to her. "How long do you have left?"

She smiled carefully. "Fifty, maybe sixty years."

"How?" I raised my eyebrows.

"Rosary made a mistake. Okay, it wasn't even a mistake. There's no way she could have known~I didn't even know it myself!"

"Mum, what are you talking about?"

She laughed. "Do you think you can get up? We can walk down into the village while we talk."

"I can try." I pulled myself up with the help of the wall, and Thorne supported me on my left side. Step by step, we walked towards the exit, while Mum started to explain.

"Back in the army, we microdosed on common poisons to get a basic immunity. It's called mithridatism. And it saved me."

"Why didn't you tell me? You could have saved us so much pain!" I said.

"If I'd known it, I'd said something, I swear!" She shook her head. "Seventeen years since the last microdose, and it still works – who would've thought that?" She hesitated. "Maybe I could have guessed. Maybe, there weren't even plants that delayed the effect – I have never heard of one, after all."

"You think it was about the microdosing too?" Thorne asked.

Mum nodded. "But even if I'd remembered it – I'd never thought it would save me. I felt shitty, after all. Up to one point down in the catacombs when I thought it was over. When I couldn't breathe anymore. And then, all of a sudden, I felt great again. Given the circumstances, that is – and then I remembered that army thing."

"So that's why you said I should leave with the book?"

"Correct. I mean, I would have told you either way, but I hoped to survive like this. Rosary wanted me to die the more painful way, so she just stabbed my arm for the scream you probably heard."

"Incredible," I mumbled. "So in the end, it all went well?"

"Almost." Mum slowly shook her head. "I can't believe Floyd is dead. If I get my hands on Cecily~"

"Nevada~" Thorne hesitated. "Didn't you~ You said you wanted to see him dead. You said you wanted to torture him, that's what you said, isn't it? But down in the cave~ Nevada, you aren't really~?"

"Siblings?" Mum laughed bitterly. "You're kidding."

"Not quite. You know, not all siblings are biological." She let out a deep sigh. "In my army time, Floyd was like a brother for me. *Like* a brother, that is. And no, actually, I never wanted to see him dead. I wanted to kill the one I made him become. The hypnosis – it was perfectly done. After seventeen years, I knew nothing about him anymore. I was convinced it was the real him." She shook her head. "On the one hand, I'm glad it wasn't. But on the other hand... his death would have been so much easier for me if he'd really hated me."

Thorne and I exchanged a look. Neither of us really knew what to say, so we walked on in silence.

I allowed the memories of the past hours to pass me by again. At least I had avoided another panic attack, another hallucination.

"I killed a man," I finally broke the silence.

Mum spun around to face me.

"I killed a man," I repeated as she didn't say anything. "In the hotel room. One of the Wickeds. Makes a great new topic for therapy, right?"

"Oh, Sparrow." Mum pulled me into a long hug. "You really are my daughter." And I was not sure if she meant it in a good or bad way.

We didn't speak of it again for days.

We had almost reached the estate exit and were just leaving the forest, when a voice made us spin around again.

"You were wrong, Nemo," a voice said from the shadows and I watched in disbelief as Cecily stepped into the clearing, a pistol in her hands.

My hand slid into my back pocket and my fingers wrapped around my gun. I knew I wouldn't be able to shoot with my left hand, but maybe she would believe it somehow.

"Not all Wickeds went with the army. I escaped, for a specific reason. I'm here because of you, Nevada Morrigane."

"Step back, kids," Mum said, softly but forcefully pushing Thorne and me a bit further away. Then she took a step forward. "What do you want? My life, after you've already taken Floyd's?"

"Why not?" She smiled for a second, but then, her façade broke. "Here, take it." She threw the gun over to Mum and knelt down. "It's long due. I understand that I have done wrong. Judge me."

"Cecily~" Mum turned the pistol in her hands. "I have done wrong too. Am I the one to judge?"

She was seriously thinking about it, of course she was. She wanted to kill Cecily. But would she?

"You have done wrong, but you were convinced it was for a greater good. I have done wrong, but it was for a selfish, pointless purpose. I killed your almost-brother and before that, I tried to kill *you*, Nemo. And if it weren't for your husband, I would have done it. You're lucky to have him." Her voice was free of spite and full of honesty and as she knelt on the ground, she just seemed broken. Nothing was left of the fighter she had previously been.

"Do it. I deserve it," she said.

Mum stared at her for a few seconds. "I know what you want me to do," she said in a cold voice. "You want me to smile, throw the gun away and help you up. You want me to say that you don't deserve to die because that you understand what you have done wrong shows that you still have a spark of decency."

Cecily glanced up at her.

"But I won't do that." Mum loaded the gun and the noise echoed through the forest. "Too many innocents died in this war. Now it's time for a guilty person to die."

"Yourself, Morrigane?" Cecily gave her a bitter look. "Oh, I forgot. You're innocent."

"I'm not innocent, Cecilia. But neither are you. I understand the wish for revenge that led you in these fights, but there's no use in an endless war that just consists of our fights for revenge. It's time to end this. The revenge I will be taking is going to be the last one in this war."

"Nemo—"

"Shut up."

"It's your right to do it."

"I don't need your permission. That you cooperate doesn't grant you my mercy. And you can be lucky the kids are here. I wouldn't have let you get away this easily otherwise." *Click.* "Mercy is overrated." *Bang.*

Silence. I felt dizzy and turned my eyes to the sky. "Oh my God, Mum, you—"

"Don't use the Lord's name in a godforsaken situation like this," Mum cut me off. "Let's leave."

"Nevada—" Thorne slowly said. "You just killed Cecily."

"I've followed every law in the war and still did everything wrong," Mum gave back. "And now I did something that was wrong *and* against the law. Cecily was right when she said there is no good and evil, just a blurring grey mess. What the LeDouxes did was wrong. What Floyd did was wrong. What Cecily did was wrong. And what I did was just as wrong, but nobody will put me into a trial for it. They will celebrate me again. For *murder.* Do you think that's right?"

It was a rhetorical question, and we kept silent.

Mum let out a deep sigh and threw the gun on the ground. "Time to leave this place forever."

MEMORIES
Jasmine

The teens in the opera house were chattering like a flock of chickens, and I couldn't blame them. Most of them had woken up from the hypnosis and now tried to comprehend what they had done. And for eleven of them, the situation was entirely new.

Had they once been awoken, been informed about life in the 21st century by the LeDouxes, so had they now regained the memories of their past life.

The return of the final missing memories of my past had hit me hard as well, and I had already known most of it – *they* hadn't had any clue until now.

Apparently, I had had a crush on the nerd and had even kissed him. Insane. Thorne Fox and Jasmine DeLuna. No thanks.

Everest, Mr. Morrigane and I stood at the edge of the stage. We had brought the involuntary fighters here after the army members had arrived to take the Wickeds to prison – they'd given in without much of a fight because they'd realised the war was senseless without the Eternals. And fairly, I assumed many of them had been under the influence of the hypnotising teens as well.

Yeah, and here we were now. I'd stood here only days ago, had hit Cecily's head with my bat, when she had revealed herself as a Wicked Magician. And within a week, she'd turned into a killing machine. I'd seen her face as she'd killed Robinett – full of *joy*.

And she, out of all people, was missing now.

Everest, Mortimer and I had brought the Wickeds here with the help of the teens – all of the Wickeds. Or so we'd thought.

Until a guy from the army had arrived from London and had asked for Cecily Williams.

Of course, we hadn't had a single calm minute afterwards. Mortimer cursed himself for leaving his wife, daughter, and Thorne alone, but at the same time, he didn't let anyone outside anymore.

Two army soldiers were sent to look for Cecily, more hadn't arrived yet.

When would they return, together with Sparrow, Thorne and Nemo?

Nevada with an odd confidence at the front, followed by Sparrow and Thorne, visibly insecure.

"Vadie!" Mr. Morrigane jumped up and ran to hug his wife. "I was so scared Cecily would find you! She managed to somehow escape and–"

"I know." Nemo sounded grim. "She found us."

I flinched. "She found you?"

"But I made sure she won't do any more harm."

Mr. Morrigane frowned. "Do you mean–"

"Mum killed her," Sparrow blurted out in a hoarse voice. "Cecily is dead!"

❧ 🕷 ☙

Cecily is dead, and the legendary Nemo killed her.

Alright.

I took a deep breath, couldn't take my eyes off of the woman in front of me. Nevada Morrigane was more than just Sparrow's loving mother. She was a killer, through and through, and never before had I been so vividly aware of this fact than in this very moment that she stood in front of me, blood drenching her clothes, shading her skin, clogging her hair, with that determined look in her eyes. She'd done what had to be done, I was sure of that.

No matter if it was morally acceptable or not.

"What are we doing here?" Nemo asked in a seemingly dismissive way, and I shuddered. Even if this was just a mask, it was scary how fast she could repress the thought of a murder.

"We brought the teens here, and the adults, and the Wickeds..." Everest's voice broke. He seemed just as devastated as I was.

"And the army isn't here yet, I assume?" Nemo smiled slightly. "But we managed to do so much without them, then we can also manage this. The Victorian teens need to be told the truth, and the formerly hypnotised people need psychological support. Telling from what Floyd said, everybody remembers what they did in their hypnotised state..." Her voice broke and even if I had yet to comprehend the connection between her and the dead army leader, I could sense her mourning.

"You could tell them a story," Mr. Morrigane said. "A story of life and death. The story of White Lilies."

"The truth I owe to the world. Yes, the story of White Lilies." Nemo smiled faintly, nodded and entered the stage, where she sat down at the edge and began to speak.

A STORY OF LIFE AND DEATH
Sparrow

"**B**ack in *2003* and *2004*, the first Arcane Magic War made the army members suffer from a scheme that was the LeDouxes' work. They made the army leaders believe that the Wickeds were evil and planned to poison the world with a so-called cure for a common disease. We didn't know that the cure was in fact nothing more than a cure, and we were told to fight them and to get that recipe and all their supplies from the potion. Lots of innocents died, many of them by my hand. And the scheme was not resolved until a few days ago, when Cecily Williams made me think about what I had really known about the backstory behind the war. So I decided to break into the army headquarters together with my daughter Sparrow, and we found out that Cecily had been right. That the army had fought for the wrong side. That I, myself, had fought for the wrong side. Unknowingly. But the army leaders knew, and had kept it a secret. I had to get that out to the public. It caused the second war we have just been through, but I just could not live alone with the knowledge about my and our guilt. The young, adventurous teenager that had been excited about fighting for the greater good has grown into a woman who regrets what she has done."

A tear ran down Mum's cheek and Dad sat down beside her to embrace her, while I turned the TV volume up to hear the interview better.

"For these wars," Mum in the TV continued in a faltering voice, *"I do not want to blame anyone but the LeDouxes. Their selfishness and vanity and their wish to not be confused with the Wicked Magicians was the cause to have the Wickeds and the army battle each other, and these old arguments were also the cause for the second war, even though Wickeds and Eternals fought on the same side, this time."*

Dad smiled, but Mum didn't smile along. They both knew what part of the interview was coming next.

"I am grateful for being given the title of a Lady and this new job – As the new army leader, I firstly want to apologise. Finally. In the name of the whole army. We have done wrong, have done things that can't be excused. And I want to ensure that in the future, the Wickeds will finally be allowed and supported to continue working on the cure they had to waive for the past twenty years. Furthermore, I am glad to develop a programme to get the Victorian teens introduced to the modern world as good as possible. We will find caring families for them."

Mum in the TV took a deep breath.

"I'm glad I have been offered the opportunity to take this new job, and I am sure I will be a more than worthy successor of Sir Floyd Robinett."

EPILOGUE
Sparrow

It was late in the evening of November 21st, 2021. My 17th birthday.

People were celebrating inside the house, while Thorne, Jasmine, Everest and I sat in the garden, gazing at the stars. Everest and his family had come specially for me from their home a good 200 hundred kilometres away.

By an odd coincidence, Jasmine's parents lived just a few villages away from our hometown and Jasmine had her fashion designer apprenticeship in the same village where Thorne and I were attending school. We even had the same therapist.

It was just Everest who lived far away from us, and we couldn't meet often, but he had insisted on returning to his family – for whom it had been even harder than for Jasmine's parents to accept the return of their dead child, but they'd managed.

White Lilies Creek had stayed a Victorian village and there were no indications that this would change any time soon.

I had killed a man, and Mum had killed a woman.

Our whole family was still regularly attending therapy.

But it was okay. At least we were all alive.

And with that thought, I laid down in the cold, dewy grass next to the others and watched stars shooting across the nocturnal sky.

One of our cats laid down on my belly and Rain nibbled my ear. With Thorne's hand in mine, everything was perfect for the moment.

LIST OF IMPORTANT CHARACTERS

Sparrow Morrigane — Thorne's girlfriend; a sacrifice of the LeDouxes who escaped last minute; daughter of Nevada and Mortimer.

Thorne Fox — Sparrow's boyfriend; has also been a sacrifice of the LeDoux family who barely managed to escape; also the son of Rosary and Kyle.

Jasmine DeLuna — victim of the LeDoux's rite in 2020, got resurrected and joined Sparrow and Thorne again

Nevada Morrigane — Sparrow's mother; an ex-warrior and now a police woman; also known as Nemo.

Mortimer Morrigane — Sparrow's father; a vet.

Cecily Williams — the ex-landlady of Thorne and Sparrow; a double agent who worked for both the Wickeds and fought in the Magic Wars for the army

Rosary LeDoux — some sort of leader of the LeDoux family clan

Clarisse LeDoux — mother of Kyle and Estelle; actually the main leader of the clan

Thill & Estelle LeDoux — members of the LeDoux family

Kyle LeDoux — husband of Rosary LeDoux; father of Ethan and Thorne

Ethan LeDoux — son of Rosary and Kyle and brother of Thorne; is a baby

Rain — unicorn squirrel buddy of Sparrow

Everest Beckett — Thorne's ex-boyfriend, got killed in a rite by the LeDouxes

Sir Floyd Richard Robinett — the leader of the magic army

THANKS

Thank you to all my friends on Instagram who helped me develop the plot and characters, gave me advice for the cover designs and for an appropriate price for this book.

A very special thanks goes to my friend, alpha & beta reader and platonic wife Mirthe. Without you, the entire White Lilies Trilogy wouldn't have ever existed in this way, and I am very sorry for all the midnight rants you had to go through XD

Another special thank you goes to my girlfriend Sina, who gives me mental stability in life lol <3

Another Thank You goes to you as the reader. Your support means the world to me!

THE AUTHOR & OTHER BOOKS BY HER

The author Janina Raven is a 17-year-old German girl. She has been writing since her early childhood and she also likes drawing, photography, graphic design, and listening to music.

In 2020 she published a novel and novella in German, which are called "Rebel School" and "Tungldraumur", as well as "White Lilies Manor", the first book of the White Lilies Trilogy. "White Lilies Creek" and the second "Rebel School" book came out in 2021.

She also appreciates book reviews on amazon or wherever you bought this book :)

You can find some bonus "White Lilies" stories, such as pieces of Nemo's backstory and her past with Floyd Robinett, on Wattpad under @janinaravensbooks!

Contact me: Instagram ~ @janina.raven.writing
Buy my merch: Redbubble ~ Raven&Duck
Check out my website ~ janinaraven.carrd.co